ISABELLA
for REAL

To Emma Ciao!

Margi Preston 2019

To Emma-Ciao!

ISABELLA for REAL

Margie Palatini

art by LeUyen Pham

HOUGHTON MIFFLIN HARCOURT
Boston   New York

hmhco.com

Text set in ITC Berkeley Oldstyle Std.

The Library of Congress has cataloged the hardcover edition as follows:
Palatini, Margie.
Isabella for real / by Margie Palatini ; illustrated by LeUyen Pham.
p. cm.
Summary: Pretending to have a much more glamorous family life,
eleven-year-old Isabella worries that her new friends at a prestigious private
school will discover that she is a "big fibbing, faking phony."
[1. Honesty—Fiction. 2. Family life—Fiction. 3. Italian Americans—Fiction.]
I. Pham, LeUyen, illustrator. II. Title.
PZ7.P1755Is 2015
[Fic]—dc23
2014048515

ISBN: 978-0-544-14846-8 hardcover
ISBN: 978-1-328-90014-2 paperback

Manufacturing in the United States
DOC 10 9 8 7 6 5 4 3 2 1
4500695579

To my dear friend Denise, whose wonderfully funny family is
a constant inspiration; and my own grandparents, parents,
aunts, and uncles, from whom I learned "point of view."
—M.P.

To Juliee, who knew me for real
—L.P.

Saturday, 10:21 a.m.
Scene 1/TAKE 1
Attic Bedroom Closet

Can an eleven-year-old go to jail for fibbing, faking, and personality perjury?

Just wondering.

10:21:06 a.m.
Scene 1/TAKE 2

"ISABELLA!"

How about eleven and seven months?

10:21:08 a.m.
Scene 1/TAKE 3

"ISABELLA!"

Eleven years, seven months, two weeks, four days, seven hours—

"ISABELLA!"

I don't know how many min—

"Is-A-bell-AH!"

Yes, she is me. Guilty. All four syllables.

Person shouting: *him.* Who's him? I mean, he . . . *He?*

Sorry. I'm mostly C minus when it comes to pronouns. Spelling. I'm way better in spelling. I was solid B at Merciful Sisters on the Mount of Small Blessings.

That's where I *used* to go to school until the place ran out of grades. I have a drawer full of forest green knee socks from kindergarten through fifth. Not as many plaid jumpers. I didn't grow much between grades three and four. Except for my nose. If I lived in Muppetland, I'd be in the same gene pool as Grover or Banana Nose Maldonado. My mother says that's an exaggeration, but catch me next to Grandpop, and it's a no-brainer I inherited schnozzola DNA from his side of the family.

Inherited: I-N-H-A-I-R . . . *E?* . . . I-N-H-A-R-I . . . *E?* . . . I-N-H-double R . . . *I* . . . *E?*

Okay, so maybe that B was a little squishy.

"ISABELLA!"

He him/him/he: Vincent. My cousin. More like my big brother—who, by the way, from now on should stay on his own side of the driveway and never ask me to help him with anything again.

It's *complicated.*

Very complicated.

Lots of moving parts—as in **BOOM**.

"Isabella? Are you going to answer to me?"

That would be *no*. As in N-O.

But if I were ever speaking to that big brother traitor, I'd be using words that would guarantee my great-grandmother making sure my mouth was on the end of a bar of green Palmolive.

(Nonni doesn't allow bad language in this house. Except, of course, if it's coming from her. Our neighbors say her vocabulary—in English and Italian—is more colorful that the biggest box of Crayola crayons. I don't know much Italian, but can say for sure, Nonni is a box of 120 when it comes to English.)

"ISABELLA! Are you coming down or not?"

Me. Closet. Not going anywhere.

. . . Unless we're talking jail.

10:24 a.m.
Scene 1/TAKE 4

"ISABELL-AAAAAAAAAAAA!"

I wonder if I could escape out my bedroom window? It worked for Mom's oldest sister. When Aunt KiKi was fifteen, she ran away from home to become an actress. She climbed down the trellis, hopped on a bus, and made it all the way into Manhattan with nobody being the wiser.

A trellis is what I need, all right . . .

Too bad Nonni took a hatchet to it after hauling Aunt Kiki back home from the corner of Broadway and Forty-Second.

"Isabella!"

Maybe I could tie sheets together? Knots have been my specialty since Uncle Babe taught me how to double-tie when I was four. I have sneakers under my bed with laces Mom's tweezers can't get loose. Thing is, even if I drop three floors without breaking a leg or squashing what's left on the tomato plants (which would be a whole other kind of mess), where would I hide out? Everybody here on Broadhead Place would turn me over to Nonni.

Or Grandma.

Or Mom.

Even without a reward. (They remember what happened to the trellis.)

What I *really* need is a getaway car . . . but I don't think I can back the old Buick out of the driveway.

Aunt Rosalie never lets me practice going in reverse.

10:25 a.m.
Scene 1/TAKE 5

"IS-A-BELL-AH! Come on . . . talk to me."

Talking is how he got me into this mess. I might not

5

talk to that big-shot college person for the rest of my whole entire life.

Cut. Edit. Delete.

What life? That's been flushed and is heading for the sewer, and I already know what an ugly stinking place that is. Trust me, I've heard stories. Poppi Flavio, my great-grandmother's third husband, who she called Number Three, had a cousin who worked in the Department of Water and Sewer Utilities for thirty-seven years. *Yes*, wastewater means exactly what it sounds like it means, and probably the reason cousin Sal used so much Old Spice, we could smell him coming up the sidewalk.

"ISABELLA! People are waiting."

Translated: Sewer. Me. Eeeuuw.

"Come on, Isabella! Where are you?"

Like I'm going to tell him *that* after he blows me out of the water on YouTube: eleven million hits in three days. I beat the piano-playing cat, which is scary. The cat has more talent. (Smaller nose, too.) It's because of Vincent and his dopey videos that all those reporters, photographers, bloggers, tweeters, nosy neighbors, five TV trucks, two police cruisers, and some guy making balloon animals are camped out across the street. I think it was the balloon guy who started chanting, "Iz-zeee! Iz-zeee!"

when the *Eyewitness News* reporter went to live remote at seven thirty.

There's a circus going on downstairs too. Almost everybody I'm related to is in the basement celebrating "stardom," including Aunt KiKi, who limo'd in from Greenwich Village in a white stretch Hummer. She swooped past the reporters (and then our furnace) making her grand entrance decked out in a purple turban and false lashes that looked like black fuzzy caterpillars glued to her eyelids.

"Isabella, dahling! Kiss kiss for Auntie! What have I been saying for eons and eons? I always knew my talent was lurking around somewhere inside you, just waiting for a glorious breakout momento! And, there he is— Vincenzo, mio caro! My amahhzzingly gifted—not to mention handsome nephew! Mark my words! The next Spielberg! Scorsese! Fellini!"

One of those *complicated* parts.

Worse, *I* helped Vincent film that part of the part.

More worse: I *am* that part of the part.

Isabella Antonelli for REAL, spelled R-E-A-L.

Which is so not the good part.

"HEY, PAPARAZZO! NEWSBOY! GET OFF MY GRASS OR I'LL *ACCESS* YOUR KEISTER RIGHT ON THE SIDE-WALK. I'M TALKING YOUR BEE-HIND, MISTER!"

My great-grandmother has incredible lung capacity for a woman her age, which Nonni tells everyone is eight more years than Lincoln's four score and seven.

"Me and Abe. Historical, baby."

Amahzzing, since most of those ninety-five years, Nonni smoked more than our backyard hibachi when Uncle Babe grills sausage. (And Mom puts the fire department on speed dial when he's anywhere near charcoal.) Until Nonni quit last February, she had puffed two packs of Chesterfield Kings a day since she was fourteen. Even though Grandpop says she's inhaled enough tar to pave the turnpike, my great-grandmother has still somehow managed to outlive three husbands, one boyfriend, and six doctors. It's also why she sounds like the man who hauls our garbage.

"HEY, MICROPHONE MAN! DID YOU HEAR ME?"

Everybody from Belleville to Weehawken and all the way through the Lincoln Tunnel just heard her.

"YOU'RE TRAMPLIN' MY PACHYSANDRA, SONNY. MOVE IT!"

(As my Grandpop says, "five will get you seven" there's probably of bunch of guys on the corner right now saying that "Sonny" is stuck in neutral because he can't stop staring at my great-grandmother's hair.)

I've seen her stop traffic in almost every aisle of the grocery store, myself.

Nonni says the color is strawberry blond, but really it's pink—like cotton candy. Same shape. Just as sticky. Over the last six decades, a whole lot of bobby pins have gone missing in that sprayed stack of teased beehive. Except for one night in 1973 when a bent hairpin ended up on the pillow of Poppi Phil. He was husband Number Two, who Nonni married back in 1957, a year after Poppi Natale (Number One) keeled over reaching into the Frigidaire for a bottle of Ballantine.

"Kerplunk. Gone like that" is how Nonni tells it.

I think that's why she tears up every time she drinks a beer with her hot dog.

(Or maybe it's from the raw onions.)

Poor Poppi Phil rolled over in bed expecting a goodnight kiss, but instead got a poke in the eye from that bobby pin. He never saw the same again. My grandma says in a way it was a blessing, as Nonni never changed her hairstyle and Poppi Two never much cared for looking at that pink beehive.

Josephine's Beauty Parlor, which has a patent on that hairstyle with everyone in the neighborhood over eighty, is where Vincent filmed Episode 3. Less than forty-eight hours ago, those close-ups of pink, lavender, and Creamsicle-colored hair already had 1,928,451 likes, which is 9 million less than each of the other half dozen episodes of Vincent's "Eggplant Wars," and the reason we all made yesterday's five o'clock news.

Six and eleven, too. Every station.

(Nonni had control of the remote. She has a quick clicker finger.)

10:41 a.m.
Scene 3/TAKE 1
Attic Bedroom Closet

Nonni complained Vincent and I stole her face time.

Believe me. If I could, I would gladly give mine back.

10:43 a.m.
Scene 4/TAKE 1
Attic Bedroom

"ISABELLA! The whole block is rocking. It's a zoo out there!"

I don't really want a bird's-eye view of my life going down the toilet, but I can only sit so long crammed behind that hamper with my legs twisted like crullers, and inhaling gym socks that should have hit the washing machine a week ago.

Whoa. The crowd is bigger than last summer at the opening of the new Dairy Queen, and the DQ was giving away free ice cream. Although, just saying, the two guys hanging around the TV truck eyeballing Mr. Colandra's

1983 baby blue Chevy Caprice look more interested in those white walls than me.

Manny the hot dog guy found a primo spot, and there's no missing Mrs. Kostopoulos, front and center behind the police sawhorses with huge binoculars hanging around her neck. She's talking to someone who looks like he dressed up for Halloween a week early. (Or maybe he's a guy from Cirque du Soleil. Not sure.) There are a lot of strange-looking people out there wearing neon-colored spandex, and none are my great-grandmother's twin sisters, Ella and Minnie, who pretty much corner the market on stretch polyester.

Oh no—leaning on what last year's hurricane left of the sycamore, arms folded and looking like he knows everything there is to know . . . Frankie Domenico. Certain people, *not me,* think he's cute because of that dimple on his chin (really?), and long eyelashes. Seriously, they are not *that* long.

And he doesn't know *everything.* He only knows part of the part of everything—and only because I had no choice but to make him part of that part.

(You don't even want to know how complicated that is.)

"We have *four* networks talking series, Izzie! *Series!* Are you hearing me? It's a freakin' phenomenon!"

Well, it's a freakin' something. And another part of the part that is *so* not good, though most people would say becoming famous overnight sounds yay-whoopee-wow good.

But it's not whoopee wow.

Very not whoopee wow.

(This is where *complicated* gets kind of messy. Like two-trains-on-the-same-track-going-in-opposite-directions messy.)

Living a double life is *not* easy.

Especially for someone who is only in sixth grade. Even I don't know how I did it, and I did it. Well, okay, I do know how I did it, but I didn't *plan* to do it. That private school with a name I can't even pronounce was all Aunt KiKi's idea. I told her, "It's too fancy. It's too far. I don't speak French." (I barely figure out Italian, and I've been listening to Nonni 24/7 my whole life.)

"Nonsense. 'For-tee-ya' will broaden your horizon. Aunt Rosalie will drive. I'll supply the French dictionary."

Then the bulldozer rolled over Mom.

"Corinne, dahling—listen to your wiser and *slightly* older sister. And don't fret one momento about the expense. KiKi has taken care of everything! After my tête-à-tête with the headmaster, I can promise you, Fortier Academy for Young Women is absolutely *the* place to provide Isabella with a stimulating atmosphere and endless opportunities to stretch her imagination."

So, there you go.

Personally, I blame mahogany.

There's way too much wood in that place, not to mention marble and more than a few gargoyles, for a girl who's been surrounded by nothing but Formica, linoleum, and six-inch statues of Saint Joseph her whole life.

All that fancy-schmancy "stimulating atmosphere" short-circuited my brain cells.

Okay . . . I don't buy that excuse, and it's my excuse.

All I know is that once those two "trains" go "boom" and everybody I know finds out I've been doing what I've been doing—there won't be enough Palmolive, Dial, or Dove left on grocery shelves across New Jersey.

Could be worse.

Nonni could haul me in front of Judge Judy . . .

"The woman's got brains, even though she has a doily hanging around her neck."

WE THOUGHT A) SHE LIVED IN A PENTHOUSE IN MANHATTAN, B) FLEW IN HER PRIVATE JET TO A CASTLE IN ENGLAND...

SHE SAID HER FATHER WAS A TOP-SECRET GOVERNMENT AGENT!

AND DON'T FORGET THE EGGPLANT! SHE SAID SHE MADE THE EGGPLANT.

EVERYONE IN SIXTH GRADE THOUGHT SHE MADE THE EGGPLANT!

WE NOMINATED HER FOR CLASS PRESIDENT!

OAKLEIGH LAWSON-NG, ANISHA PATEL
X-NEW BESTIE #2, X-NEW BESTIE #3

JUDGE! SHE SWIPED MY RECIPE AND TWO PANS OF EGGPLANT PARMIGIANA!

CONSTANZA CASATI MARCHIONI PINCELLI SURIANO
GREAT-GRANDMOTHER OF ALLEGED FIBBER, FAKER, PHONY.

IN OTHER WORDS, YOUNG LADY, YOU ARE A FIBBING, FAKING, EGG-PLANT-PLAGIARIZING, FABRICATING, PHONY FULL OF BALONEY.

I'M GOING TO HAVE TO LOOK UP "FABRICATING" IN THE DICTIONARY.

WELL... WHEN YOU SAY IT LIKE THAT, IT DOES SORT OF SOUND LIKE ME.

ALTHOUGH...

I'M STILL WORKING ON VOCABULARY.

OH, AND YOUR HONOR?

I'M PRETTY POSITIVE I SAID VILLA IN ITALY, NOT CASTLE IN ENGLAND.

BAILIFF, BRING ME A TOWEL.

MY LEG IS WET.

TOLD YOU IT WAS MESSY.

10:58 a.m.
Scene 5/TAKE 1
Attic Bedroom

Here's the problem with Judge Judy:

A person only gets a measly fifteen minutes to plead her case, and I have at least an hour of complicated explaining. Not counting commercial interruptions.

"ISABELLA!"

Or Vincent.

Extremely short version:

Madeline (the book, not the cookie).

New school.

New girls.

No friends.

Want friends.

Cucumber sandwiches.

Suits of armor.

Chandeliers.

Something or somebody named Earl Grey.

Aunt KiKi going diva on the grand staircase—a capella.

(My aunt gets carried away when lots of steps are involved. When I was seven, she broke into a chorus of "Don't Cry for Me Argentina" outside the Metropolitan Museum of Art. Luckily I was able to drag "Evita" inside before Security showed up and escorted us to the sidewalk.)

And, oh . . . one more important thing: Don't believe everything you see or read on the Internet.

"ISABELLA! If you're not coming down—I'm coming up!"

11:01 a.m.
Scene 6/TAKE 1
Under the Bed

That's right. I'm hiding under my bed. I've got a small room. I'm out of options.

News Flash: If there's a contest for finding the most dust bunnies, I win.

News Flash Number Two: Beat-up old knotted sneakers smell no better than unwashed gym socks.

11:23 a.m.
Scene 7/TAKE 1

Is "quiet" good or bad?

I'm not hearing Vincent coming up the stairs, and that

would be hard to miss because our house is older than Nonni and almost every floorboard creaks, even muffled by carpet. That's also not taking into consideration the genes Vincent inherited from the big-feet side of our family. (Uncle Marty wears size 17½, and he's only five foot eight.)

Oh no. Did he go outside? Is he talking to those reporters again?

I inch out from under the bed then crawl to the window, crouching low to where my nose touches the sill. I give a peek to down below in the front yard, but don't see Vincent anywhere. More good news: I don't have to worry about vacuuming under my bed. My T-shirt mopped the dust bunnies.

Not such good news (besides a T-shirt needing a whole lot of Clorox), Frankie is still across the street sitting on the curb. Looking up at my window and grinning, yes, grinning, as he eats a Texas wiener—which, wow, smells delicious even all the way up here with the window closed.

All right, so maybe I don't actually smell that chilidog, but my stomach is growling like I can. Before making a beeline for the closet, I should have grabbed some biscotti from the kitchen table even if Aunt Rosalie was the one who baked them. Her cookies are bricks, but I'm so hungry a brick is better than no brick. Nonni's boyfriend, Mr. Schimlitz, would disagree. That is, if he were *alive* to agree. (Another story.)

I dip under the window, take the three steps to my bedroom door, and open it a crack, listening for Vincent. The problem is, I can't tell if Big Foot is on the move because somebody in the house just cranked up Frank Sinatra loud enough for Nonni's twin sisters to hear two houses away, and those two blew out their eardrums thirty years ago listening to Springsteen.

Frank Sinatra is the person who sings "New York, New York" after a Yankees game. (Not for real, of course. He's as dead as all my poppies and Mr. Schimlitz.) Nonni has a photograph of him hanging on the wall in the upstairs hallway, along with one President Eisenhower, two Ronald Reagans, four Joe DiMaggios, a velvet Elvis, my three dead great-grandfathers, and Arthur Schimlitz. (Poppi Two is the one with the eyepatch.)

"Whoa! Hey! Ow!"

My bedroom door bangs me square on the nose.

"Frankie! What are you doing up here?"

No. Frankie Domenico in my *room?* In this house? Never. Even if he figured a way to get in here (and I wouldn't put that past him), he'd never make it beyond the first step, creaking or no creaking. Nonni doesn't al-

21

low Jeffrey up here, and he's been my best friend since day one, when the Levandowskis moved next door eight years ago.

This Frankie is my cat. Named after not you-know-who but the singing dead one.

"Come over here, Anchovy Breath."

I pick him up before he starts scratching the carpet. Those sharp little front claws have already shredded a bare spot on the other side of my bed. I've been covering it up with a wastepaper basket. So far Aunt Rosalie and Mom, who take turns on the did-you-make-your-bed check, haven't noticed my carpet going bald or asked what a waste can is doing in the middle of the room. I'm hoping they think I've become suddenly neat-obsessed or practicing creative interior decorating for extremely small rooms.

I check in the mirror for a ballooning nose (which thankfully isn't), and the little whisker face nuzzles me under my chin. I sit down on the bed, Frankie cradled under one arm, his sandpaper tongue licking my wrist. I give him a little smooch behind his left ear, the one that got personal with the Popoviches' dog, Boomer, right before I found him last November. In this neighborhood it's no secret, that mutt is one mean pooch. I've seen what his teeth do to a soccer ball. Serious deflation. He's also a rude sniffer, if you know what I mean.

When I found this little guy, he was fur and bones, standing in garbage juice behind one of the trash cans on the side of our garage. He smelled worse than he looked, shaking and shivering so much, his stripes moved like hologram stickers on my first grade notebook.

Even though from the time I was four Nonni has always said "NO STRAY CATS IN THIS HOUSE—AND I MEAN EVAH!" no way was I leaving him outside, chewed and shivering. (Besides, *technically* he was more kitten than cat.) Mom's expert first aid, because she's the best ER nurse at the medical center, got the ear back in shape. Best she could, anyway, without gluing on the missing fur. *That* part of Frankie had already made its way through Boomer's digestive tract and was no doubt stinking up a patch of grass that passes for a front lawn on our block. Or more likely, plopped on somebody's sidewalk. (The Popoviches don't scoop.)

Six baths and half a bottle of Dawn dish detergent later, Frankie finally didn't smell too bad. After a couple of weeks Nonni even got to like him. (Although she still pushed him off her Barcalounger and made me promise in front of Jesus on the cross above her bed that I would clean the litter box every day without fail.) I promised, even though I will never ever like cleaning kitty poop. But I do love Frankie—the *cat,* of course.

"Isn't that right, Mr. Sardine Man? You were there when Vincent asked me to help him make his dumb videos, weren't you? You know how this whole big mess started, don't you?"

I turn him over and rub his now fat, furry stomach. (He really likes to chow down on Nonni's linguini.) He makes with the sleepy eyes and turns on the purr machine, which has one loud motor.

"Frankie, you remember what I told Vincent, don't you? You remember, right, Frankie? . . . Frankie? Uh, that's your cue to agree with me, Fuzz Face."

I stop the belly massage and we go eye to eye.

"*What?* You're not saying what happened is *my* fault, are you? . . . Are you?"

"Meow."

Besides breath that needs more than a few Tic Tacs, this cat obviously lacks a good memory.

Seven Months Ago

I was minding my own business . . .

It was spring break at Merciful Sisters.

I was hanging around downstairs in our basement, waiting for Jeffrey to come back from his ten thirty orthodontist appointment. We had plans: Day Two of March Madness Monopoly Marathon. We've been having the tournament every year since we were seven. He's the ship. I'm the shoe. He's the banker. I hold the properties. And we *do* put money in Free Parking. Some people say that isn't playing by the rules, but Jeffrey and I call it winning the lottery. Same as Grandpop did two years ago when he hit the five-hundred-dollar jackpot with a scratch-off ticket.

It's a good deal for Jeffrey, because he always buys Mediterranean and Baltic. Seriously, who buys those purples? No way is he ever going to win collecting four dollars. It's a mystery how Jeffrey lacks basic Monopoly killer strategy, because when it comes to everything else, especially anything on a computer, Boy Genius is like my aunt says, *amahzzing*. (He got a full scholarship to Saint Peter's Prep.)

However, just because Jeffrey is way smart didn't mean I was going to let him pass Go and collect two hundred dollars without a fight. As soon as those rubber bands were adjusted, it was game on over at his house, and my plan was to show no mercy.

I finished my chores, which since I was old enough to hold a dust rag are Windexing everything that needs a wipe of ammonia. That's plenty, since most of the furniture in the upstairs living room is slipcovered in plastic and everybody in this house is big on disinfectant.

Mom was doing a double shift at the hospital, and Aunt Rosalie had driven Nonni for her monthly *"hot-cha-cha"* manicure over at Josephine's. (Her "signature color" is baby pink.) I was home alone, except for Uncle Babe.

As usual, he was in the jalousie porch, the little room off the upstairs parlor. That's where he watches TV, the one with the rabbit-ears antenna. The old set doesn't get many channels, but when Uncle Babe bends one ear to the right and hangs a piece of aluminum foil on the other, his favorite Popeye cartoons come in all the way from Philadelphia. Most times the picture has a little "snow," but my uncle doesn't mind. He likes winter.

The basement was quiet except for a load of bath towels thumping through the washing machine spin cycle. I turned on the Game Show Network and stretched out on the couch all cozy under Aunt Rosalie's crocheted zigzag afghan, smelling like "outdoor meadow" with a hint of lemon. While I was dusting the coffee table, I figured I'd spritz myself with some of that Pledge, too. (If you ask me, it smells better than Aunt Rosalie's perfume.)

I had already polished off a strawberry jelly sandwich and was doing serious damage to a bag of Cheddar Jalapeño Cheetos, my favorite breakfast when nobody is around to stop me, while Frankie (not *him*) and I played along with the contestants on *Match Game*.

"Dumb Dora is so dumb she _____ the coffee."

The idea of this show is to fill in the blank with a funny answer, so I said "fried," which was near brilliant, because I got five matches and was going for the Big Money Bonus Round. The emcee holding the skinny microphone had just spun the Star Wheel when I heard Vincent and his big feet coming down the cellar stairs and through the kitchen. As he cleared the corner by the refrigerator, I could see he was wearing sunglasses, even though there was no sun, Grandpop's old houndstooth fedora, and a three-day stubble. He was also carrying the video camera Aunt KiKi had bought him when he started film school last September.

"Uh, Vincent, would you move out of the way there, please? You're blocking Charles Nelson Reilly. I'm about to win mucho dinero."

"How can you watch this? It's from a zillion years ago."

"Not a zillion. Hey, don't sit next to me! Now look what you did—you made Frankie run under the recliner. Oooh—quick!—check out that guy with the mustache and sideburns: he's wearing Uncle Babe's orange plaid jacket!"

"Quit being a couch potato and hand over the remote. Enough of 1974."

"It's *Match Game 75*."

We played keep-away. Vincent always wins. (No fair. His arms are longer.) He clicked, the TV went black, and I never found out if I matched Chuck and won the big money.

Vincent slipped one stem of his sunglasses down the neck of his black sweatshirt and shook his head. "You're getting time-warped watching this stuff."

"You live next door my whole life, and *now* you think I'm warped? My brain is buckled more than the linoleum floor. I'm the only person in this house besides Mom under seventy-three years old. I don't even have to read a history book. I hear everything firsthand. Did you know in 1933 a roll of toilet paper cost four cents?"

"Well, there's a fascinating insignificant detail for you. I'll make a note of that."

"I've got another one—ketchup wasn't even a dime. A whole bottle."

"Stop with the grocery list, sit up, and ditch the blanket. Look at yourself—covered up to your chin like Aunt Rosalie."

"I'm comfy."

"Comfy. What are you, seventy-five? Next I'll find you knitting one of these things."

"It's not knitting. Crochet. You use one hook, not two needles."

"*You* are scaring me. Give me this blanket."

"Afghan."

He tugged. I tugged. But Vincent won the battle and tossed it to the other side of the couch.

"Shorts?" he said, tapping my bare knees. "What are you doing wearing shorts in March?"

"Nonni turned up the furnace to 'roast.' When I woke up this morning, I thought I was in Florida."

Vincent laughed. "Perfect. See, that's exactly what I'm looking for."

"What do you mean, what you're looking for? Uh-oh. You're after something."

"Listen to suspicious you. I'm just looking for a little help, that's all."

Vincent was suddenly sounding like he could sweeten the coffee Aunt Rosalie brews, which should have warned me that nothing good was coming from whatever he wanted: In a blindfold taste test between my aunt's coffee and mud, mud wins every time.

"Come on, Isabella. Help me."

I popped a Cheeto into my mouth. "Sorry. Can't. Busy."

"You're not busy."

"Am."

"Not."

"Am. Monopoly with Jeffrey as soon as he comes home—so goodbye."

"Hey! Stop blocking my lens with those orange cheesy fingers!" He dropped the camera to one hip and got all sugary again. "Come on. What do you say? I really need you, Isabella. I want an A in my film course this semester. Help me out here, huh?"

I mussed my hair, lifted my chin, and threw my head back. "But how can *I* rhally, rhally help you, Vincenzo, *dahling*," I said in a deep, low voice. "I'm not an ahck-triss like Ahhnt KiKi."

He laughed. "Pretty good. You almost sound just like her."

"Really?"

"No."

"Yes I do," I said, playfully swatting his arm. "Let me pretend I'm Aunt KiKi. I can do it."

"That's what I'm afraid of," he said with another chuckle. "Look, I want you to be *you*. No acting. Especially not like Aunt KiKi."

Nobody acts or sounds like Aunt KiKi.

Even KiKi didn't act and sound like KiKi until after waiting tables and doing bit parts on Off-Broadway for years and years, she landed the role of Contessa Francesca Monchetti on the soap opera *Search for Truth, Lies and Love*.

As I was barely three at the time and spending afternoons in playpen captivity facing the TV, I watched the show every day with Grandma, Aunt Rosalie, and Nonni. Never missed an episode, even when I was long past the sippy cup and finally sprung from the pen. Actually, I followed the plot way better than they could. By the time I turned seven it was my job to fill them in on what was happening when they couldn't figure it out themselves, which was most of the time, as The Contessa had a very complicated story line (including more dead husbands than my great-grandmother).

She also had a long-lost daughter *and* a long-lost son; tumbled down a flight of stairs and woke up from a coma believing she was an opera star; was poisoned with espresso by the evil Baron Cieri and her even more evil twin sister, who were planning to steal her fashion empire; and time-traveled back to 1915 and sank with the *Lusitania*.

Believe me, it wasn't easy explaining to Nonni why there weren't actually two KiKis or how she came back from the dead. (She had already made funeral arrangements.)

The show made my aunt *kind* of famous. (Not red-carpet famous, although she has one in her apartment, where she practices walking just in case that ever happens.) And even though the show was canceled three years ago, she still receives lots of fan mail—bags and bags.

The thing is, those letters aren't addressed to KiKi Caruso, but to "The Contessa." My aunt calls them her "most devoted fans." The "intensely devoted" ones have even made what Aunt KiKi calls "worship websites." Those fans believe Francesca Monchetti is not a character on a soap opera but an actual real person. Which is why when anyone comes up to my aunt, even in a restaurant ladies' room while she's washing her hands, and says, *"Aren't you Francesca Monchetti?"* Aunt KiKi reaches for a marker (she keeps one handy for just such occasions), pulls a paper towel from the dispenser, and signs "Contessa."

"Remember, dahling," she always tells me, *"never intentionally destroy the reality of devoted fans."*

I batted my eyes. "So tell me again, *Vincenzo, dahling,* why don't you want me to act like Ahhnt KiKi?"

Vincent panned the room with the camera and caught Frankie sneaking out from under the recliner and making a dash for the furnace.

"I told you. I want you to be *you.*"

"Me, is boring. I'm a couch potato, remember? And besides, I think I'm getting a pimple right here," I said, pointing to my chin. "I don't want people seeing me with my very first zit."

"That's not a pimple, you little goof—it's jelly. And what people? I told you, this is a project for my film course. The only person ever seeing this mockumentary is my professor."

"Mock-u-what? I don't get it."

"You don't have to get it. Just be my adult in the room."

"I'm eleven."

"That's the point. You're my voice of reason. Or will be—after I edit. You won't believe the footage I got yesterday at my house. Grandma comes down for breakfast and starts arguing with Grandpop about who put the spoon in the fork drawer. Grandpop tells her he never uses a spoon. And says it while eating Cheerios. Grandma then dumps all the silverware from the kitchen drawer into the garbage. Including the drawer. Golden. Absolutely golden."

"Uh-huh." I yawned and plumped up one of Aunt Rosalie's crocheted pillows. "Spoon. Fork drawer. Garbage. What else have you got? 'Who squeezed the toothpaste tube in the middle?' 'Where did you put the *TV Guide*?'"

"Are you helping me or not?"

"I'll think about it," I said, reaching into the bottom of the bag and snagging another Cheeto.

Before I had a chance to crunch, Vincent grabbed my arm and pulled me off the couch. "I knew you wouldn't let me down. Come on. Let's film Uncle Babe. I'll follow you upstairs. Point out anything interesting along the way."

"*Interesting?* Vincent. Hello. This is Nonni's house."

"See? What you said—how you said it? *Attitude*. That's exactly what I'm looking for. And I love that eyebrow thing you do. Totally works."

"I do an eyebrow thing?"

Must have inherited that from Aunt KiKi. She always

lifted one eyebrow as the camera zoomed in for a close-up right before the commercial break.

Since I was still waiting around for Jeffrey, and Vincent promised nobody was ever seeing these stupid videos but his professor, I wiped the jelly off my chin and let him follow me around the house. Vincent filmed. I pointed. Made comments. Did the eyebrow thing. I also negotiated one sweet deal: I help him with his videos and he's on the hook for an open tab at Holsten's. That place has the best burgers and homemade ice cream for miles around. I always order the double cheese with a side of rings and a pineapple shake. Jeffrey orders his double with cheese fries and gets a sundae with four scoops any flavor, chocolate sauce, and whipped cream.

Grandpop would say Jeffrey and I came way out ahead on that deal.

AND WE'RE ROLLING...

ACTION!

WORKING TITLE:
EGGPLANT WARS
ROUGH FOOTAGE

SO HERE WE ARE IN WHAT MY FAMILY CALLS THE "LOWER FIRST FLOOR"--OR WHAT EVERYBODY ELSE CALLS THE BASEMENT.

THIS IS THE CELLAR KITCHEN. COOL IN THE SUMMER. NICE AND TOASTY IN THE WINTER.

WHEN YOUR CHAIR IS AT THE END OF THIS KITCHEN TABLE, THE GUY NEXT TO YOU IS THE OIL FURNACE.

THIS GREEN MONSTER MAY BE THE SIZE OF A VOLKSWAGEN BEETLE AND HISSES LIKE ONE OF ITS LEAKING TIRES WHEN THE HEAT KICKS ON ...

BUT IT'S A HANDY HOTPLATE IF YOUR FOOD GETS COLD.

CUT!

ROLLING!

NO COOKING IS EVER DONE IN THE UPSTAIRS KITCHEN.

THE OVEN IN THIS OLD NORGE IS WHERE NONNI, GRANDMA, AND AUNT ROSALIE HIDE THEIR POCKETBOOKS.

IT'S SORT OF THEIR SAFE.

EXCEPT LAST SUMMER THE POCKETBOOKS WEREN'T SO SAFE, BECAUSE UNCLE BABE THOUGHT HE WAS WARMING UP A MEATBALL SANDWICH BUT INSTEAD ENDED UP ROASTING THREE LEATHER HANDBAGS.

NEIGHBORS FOUR BLOCKS AWAY HEARD THE SMOKE ALARM. MOM EMPTIED THREE CANS OF SPRUCE AIR FRESHENER, BUT THE WHOLE HOUSE STILL SMELLED OF SMOKED POCKETBOOK MARINARA.

ACTUALLY, SMOKED POCKET BOOK MARINARA HANGING ON CHRISTMAS TREE.

WITH BURNT MOZZARELLA

IF YOU TAKE A DEEP BREATH, YOU CAN STILL GET A FAINT WHIFF OF COOKED HANDBAG AND SPRUCE TREE FLOATING AROUND THE HOUSE.

CUT!

11:31 a.m.
Scene 9/TAKE 1
Attic Bedroom

"You don't remember any of that, Sardine Breath, because you bailed and high-tailed it under the furnace."

Frankie looks at me and yawns.

"Guess somebody is also forgetting who saved a certain cat from getting tossed out the door when he crawled out looking more gray than orange and got a bath before Nonni caught sight of him."

Frankie wets his whiskers and starts pawing his face clean.

"Look, Frankie . . . I was only trying to help Vincent get an A. How did I know when we filmed those dopey things in March that six months later he was going decide to upload, download, and unload everything on YouTube? Without even telling me!

"See . . . here's the thing, Frankie . . . if it weren't for those videos of me being me going viral, it wouldn't really matter that I'd told a couple of little fibs to Emory, Oakleigh, and Anisha . . . right?

"I mean . . . all *I* did was let them think what they were already thinking. What's so wrong about that? I only wanted them to like me. And they did. They do. They really like that other Isabella. Frankie? . . . Excuse me, but yawning in my face is extremely rude. And stinky."

He rolls over, curls his toes, and stretches his back legs. He blinks, stands up, and jumps off the bed.

"Hey, wait a minute, Tuna Fish Face," I say, watching him head for the door. "Frankie? . . . Where are you going?"

Things are not looking good when your own cat walks out on you.

11:36 a.m.
Scene 10/TAKE 1

"Isabella! Wherever you're hiding, listen up: Interview with *Access Today* this afternoon. It's all set. Be at my house one o'clock."

Interview with *me?* Being me? As in the real me?

Not happening. I can't have one more picture of my face plastered somewhere else before I get a chance to explain to my friends why I did what I did.

Of course, I haven't thought of what a good explanation of that would be just yet.

"One o'clock, Isabella! Be there or I'm coming to get you. And you know I'll find you."

He's not lying. I was never able to fool him when we played hide-and-seek. Of course, Vincent has eight years on me and back then I was only four. I would think by now I should be able to come up with a hiding place less obvious than under the kitchen table or rolled up in one of Aunt Rosalie's afghans.

I hope.

"Did you hear me?"

I've got to get out of here. And fast. I can't do interviews. I have to figure out how to unfib six weeks of whoppers before school starts Monday morning and I come face-to-face-to-face with Emory, Oakleigh, and Anisha.

I smell onions and peppers.

I'm making a run for it.

That aroma coming up the stairs means *second helpings*, which means it's a no-brainer Vincent is in the basement stuffing an egg sandwich into his mouth, and nowhere

44

near the bottom of the stairs. It's my best chance to break out through the kitchen door.

(I ruled out the window. A trellis is pretty much essential when you're dropping from anywhere higher than the first floor, and I'm kind of iffy about shimmying down the drainpipe. Last year in gym class I aced rope climbing going up but was never quite A material on the way down.)

The new plan is not only simpler and safe—it's also totally foolproof. As Aunt Rosalie says when she boils water, "easy peasy."

In this house eating is a very noisy activity. If chewing were an Olympic sport, my family would win gold. Plus, fresh rolls from Manuchi's Bakery are very, very crunchy. With all the chewing, crunching, and burping, not counting other emissions from Uncle Babe, no way any of them will be hearing me on the stairs, escaping out the back door, or heading across the driveway to hide out at Aunt Minnie and Auntie Ella's house. Those two talk more than question, and only hear half the answers.

Besides, I am starving, and nobody feeds you like Aunt Minnie.

Don't tell Nonni I said that.

Halfway down the attic stairs, I put the brakes on the high-tops when I hear slippers shuffling and padding their way to the bathroom at the end of the second-floor hallway.

It sounds like Uncle Babe made it past Velvet Elvis and stalled somewhere between Joe DiMaggio and Poppi Natale.

I wait.

Three more shuffle-slides and I hear the bathroom door open.

Close.

The lock clicks.

No time to lose. Uncle Babe is the quick one in the family when it comes to spending time in that particular room. Depending how many cups of coffee he drank with his sandwich, I have one minute—two, tops—to make it downstairs and out the back door. I make a quick turn on the second-floor landing and race down to the first floor.

The toilet flushes.

The bathroom door opens.

Slippers shuffle again down the hallway. I swing

46

around the newel post, hurdle over the ottoman, fire the second booster on my Chucks through the dining room, and make it into the kitchen before the stairs start creaking under Uncle Babe's feet. I tap the front burner of the Norge for good luck and reach for the knob on the back door.

From the basement I hear Aunt KiKi doing a duet with dead Frank Sinatra. She's trying her best to compete with Grandma and Grandpop, who are arguing about which one of them used the last drop of half-and-half, but is losing big-time. (My aunt can really belt out a song, but it's Grandma who inherited Nonni's lung power.) I push open the storm door, hoping my grandparents aren't blaming Frankie for lapping up the cream.

Yes, that would be the cat.

A gust of wind and the faint aroma of chilidogs hits my face as I jump off the cement porch and land on the worn-down path of grass leading to the driveway. I dash to the corner of the house. I part a bunch of dried flowers hanging on the hydrangea bush and peek toward the street, making sure the coast is clear.

I gulp.

Walking down our driveway, heading straight in my direction—Frankie.

That would *not* be the cat.

11:44 a.m.
Scene 13/TAKE 1
The Backyard

I know some choice words that for sure would have me eating soapsuds, but don't have time to say them. Frankie's swaggering stroll is picking up the pace, and I've got nowhere to hide.

Standing behind the trunk of the maple is not going to do it, since the tree is skinnier than I am. Nonni's lawn statue of the Virgin Mary is way too short, and I don't think I can make it into the garage without Frankie seeing me. No room in there anyway; that's where Aunt Rosalie stores her boxes of Christmas decorations. She has more than 350 Christmas villages piled up to the rafters. (My aunt is sort of QVC-obsessed. Which is why she's on a first-name basis with the UPS driver.)

The garbage can is only a few feet away, but trash diving is *not* a consideration. That would be more dangerous than dropping out the window without a trellis. Even three cans of spruce air-freshener wouldn't do the job after hiding out with the clamshells from last night's linguini.

48

Out front, someone on the street calls Frankie's name. He turns and I bolt for the Buick. Ducking behind the front grille and crouching close to the cracked macadam, I squeeze into the space between the garage door and right headlight. Since two years ago when Aunt Rosalie accidentally shifted into drive instead of reverse, she now leaves a little extra room between the car and the garage door. (I won't describe what two front tires can do to a couple of carolers and three snowmen.)

I peek over the hood ornament, careful Frankie doesn't see me, and watch as he turns for the back door of the house. I scoot around to the passenger side of the car, yank open the door, belly flop onto the front bench seat, roll under the big blue dashboard, and cross my fingers that you-know-who isn't smart enough to peek inside the LeSabre.

11:44:12 a.m.
Scene 14/TAKE 1
Aunt Rosalie's 1985 Metallic Blue Buick LeSabre

He isn't.

(I knew that.)

11:44:22 a.m.
Scene 14/TAKE 2
Under the Dashboard of the Buick

My heart is thumping.

My hands are sweating.

I haven't been this nervous since in the summer when I was getting ready to attend the Fortier Welcome Tea.

That Fateful Hot Day in August

"I look like Madeline," I said, choking through the stiff tight collar of the blouse. (Nonni got carried with the spray starch). "I look better in plaid."

"Nonsense. You look mahhvelous, dahling!" Aunt KiKi insisted as she straightened my red necktie, while I sweated under the gray blazer. "This touch of color does wonders for you. *Très chic*."

"I don't feel tray sheik," I groaned as my stomach made another awful-sounding gurgle, and I reached across the kitchen counter for the bottle of Pepto Bismol.

"Mark my words. This school will be a whole new adventure for you."

I unscrewed the cap and for the second time since breakfast and took a swig of the pink stuff. "I think I hate adventure," I said with burp.

"What are you talking about, dahling? You adored the trip down the Amazon."

I rolled my eyes. "Aunt KiKi, I was watching from the couch and that river was a set in a studio on Long Island."

"Well, those lights were hot enough for me to believe I was in a Brazilian jungle. Reality is nothing but perception, dahling. Remember that."

"My perception is your hair could use a good spritz from my can of Extra Hold," interrupted Nonni, as she attacked me with a jumbo can of White Rain.

"Spinach. Our girl needs a fortifying green vegetable," said Uncle Babe, opening the refrigerator door.

"Everyone relax. Isabella is fine," Mom said, giving me a hug.

"I'm the *new* girl, Mom. Being the new girl is never 'fine.'"

"Stop worrying, dahling. Everyone at Fortier will think you're fabulous."

I sighed. "Aunt KiKi, I keep telling you, the only thing I come close to being 'semi' fabulous at is catching pop flies."

"My Swee' Pea isn't lying," Uncle Babe said with a wide grin. "I taught her everything she knows. Now that Jeter is retired, the Yanks could use her as a shortstop."

Out on the driveway, Aunt Rosalie started honking the horn on the Buick. I took one last gulp of Pepto, trudged up the basement steps and gave the old stove a tap for good luck before heading out the back door.

Mom and Aunt KiKi watched me climb into the back

seat and buckle up just as the air conditioning kicked in and started blowing my hair in every direction. (So much for "extra hold.")

"Remember what Auntie told you, dahling—Stretch! Create! Be fabulous!"

"Be *you*!" Mom called as the LeSabre eased out of the driveway.

The ride to school felt like hours, not ten minutes. (My stomach agreed.) And when we chugged up the long drive of Fortier Academy, the muffler spitting smoke as we passed each lollipop-shaped tree, I definitely knew I wasn't in Belleville anymore. (And for sure Uncle Babe wasn't doing the hedge trimming.)

Before we made it up to the circular drive and entrance steps with gargoyles staring down at me from three stories above, I should have ducked behind the front seat and told Aunt Rosalie to floor the gas pedal, and keep going until we crossed back into Belleville.

But I didn't.

BONJOUR!

ACCUEIL À L'ORIENTATION À L'ACADÉMIE DE FORTIER.

UH...OH...UM...SURE...YES! MERCY?

EQUESTRIAN CAMP WAS AWESOME.

MY FENCING INSTRUCTOR SAID I SHOW INCREDIBLE IMPROVEMENT.

MON ÉTÉ ÉTAIT FANTASTIQUE.

BE POLITE. BE FRIENDLY. BE YOURSELF.

EXPLORE! CREATE! IMAGINE! STRETCH!

AUNT KIKI

MOM

DUE TO TECHNICAL DIFFICULTIES
BEYOND OUR CONTROL,
WE ARE ONLY ABLE TO BRING
YOU AUDIO PORTIONS OF THIS
REMAINING FLASHBACK.

"Bonjour!"

I spun around and saw three girls with perfect hair, perfect teeth, and perfect unbitten nails.

It was going to be harder for me to fit in than I thought. My stomach gurgled. I burped. (And it wasn't only because of that cucumber sandwich I'd just swallowed.)

"Oh . . . uh . . . sure. *Wee!* I mean bond. Boon. Bone?" I sighed in exasperation. "Ciao?"

"Hear that?" said the shoulder-tapping girl to the one wearing red glasses.

She stepped this way, the other two that way, and before I knew it I was surrounded by a trio of Madelines.

"She said *ciao*. Told you it had to be *her.*" The girl with long blond hair turned to me and smiled, showing teeth that were as straight as Jeffrey's since he got his braces removed. "I'm Emory Easton."

"Oakleigh" is how the girl in red glasses introduced herself. "Oakleigh Lawson-Ng."

"Anisha Patel," said the third, with a slight British accent.

Be friendly. Be polite. (Try not to think you look completely doofy wearing this red necktie, even if you do.)

"You don't mind if we talk to you, do you?" whispered Oakleigh, curling a short strand of dark hair around one ear.

"Mind? Me? No. I was only talking to Sir Lancelot here."

"Hey, she's funny! I like her!" said Anisha. "Tell us you play soccer. We so need a good defender!"

"Soccer? I'm okay, I guess. Better at softball."

"Fabulous! We also need a shortstop who can field. Consider yourself on the team!"

(Maybe fitting in wasn't going to be as difficult as I thought.) I took a deep breath and smiled. "I guess you figured out I'm the 'new girl' here. I'm . . . uh . . . I'm actually pretty good at catching pop flies."

"Isabella, right?" said Emory.

"You *are*, aren't you?" said the girl.

"Of course it's her, Oakleigh," Anisha said, flipping her long, dark French braid behind her shoulder. "It *has* to be her."

"Her?" I said. "I mean, me? She? . . . You *know* me?"

Emory leaned closer and whispered, "We do. Your *mom*, too."

I blinked. "*My* mom?"

(Did she mean from the hospital emergency room? None of these three girls looked like she had any recent broken bones or needed a blood transfusion.)

"Sorry, Isabella," Oakleigh quickly apologized as the

other two nodded in synchronized agreement. "We know your mom gave the office strict instructions to keep both your identities secret."

"She did?"

(I thought all Mom did was put her name on the admission papers Aunt KiKi brought her to sign.)

Anisha finished a last bite of cucumber sandwich and crumpled the paper napkin into her fist. "Don't fret, Isabella. You can trust us. We promise not to breathe a solitary word about what we know."

"Totally promise," Emory said, crossing her heart.

Granted, my brain and stomach weren't exactly working in sync just now, but I was feeling something was not right here besides my gurgling gut.

"Uhhhh . . . I think you have me mixed up with somebody else. I'm Isabella Anton—"

"*Antonelli.* We know," whispered Oakleigh, glancing over her shoulder and scanning the groups of girls nearby for eavesdroppers. "We're lifers at Fortier," she said, turning back to me.

"Lifers?"

"Been here since pre-K. We have *sources.*"

"That's how we *know* what we *know,*" said Anisha, in a voice I could barely hear.

Never mind understanding French. I had no idea what these girls were saying in English. "What *exactly* do you know?" I whispered back.

Emory raised an eyebrow to Oakleigh and Anisha. "She's *good.*"

"She's very good," agreed Oakleigh.

"Isabella, you can relax. We know all about keeping things low-key. Fortier Academy is loaded with famous people—just like you."

I stepped back and bumped into Lancelot. "Did you say . . . like *me?*"

"There are three girls in eighth, one in second, and two in third who have dads who are Giants and Devils—not the beanstalk or horns-and-pitchfork types, but—"

"Oakleigh means football and hockey players," Anisha interrupted as Oakleigh rolled her eyes up toward the enormous beamed ceiling. "And Tanya Buchanan—she's a junior in the upper school—her mother is a big-deal congresswoman. And of course, can't forget Brittany Lockwood. Her dad is 'Lock and Load,' the Storage King. He owns more than one thousand franchises all across the country. But of course, he's not *real* royalty like *your* mum."

"*Royalty* like my 'mum'?" I almost coughed up that cucumber sandwich.

"Are you all right, Isabella? Have a sip of Earl Grey," Anisha said, offering her cup.

Oakleigh whispered, "We've been wondering, what exactly do we call a daughter of a *countess*?"

"What?" I said, dribbling tea down my necktie.

"Not countess, Oakleigh," Emory corrected. "Isabella's mother is a *contessa*."

I bumped back into Lancelot again. "Ow . . . Ouch . . . N-n-n-no!" I handed the teacup back to Anisha and held up both hands in front of me. "Whoa. There's been some sort of mix-up here. My mother isn't a contessa!"

Anisha put her fingers to her lips. "We understand it, Isabella. We know all about how she wants her identity kept *secret*."

Emory glanced over one shoulder, checking for eaves-droppers, then put her hand on my arm and leaned close. "*Our* source heard from another source who was told by a certain excellent source who got it straight from *the* most *impeccable* source there is at Fortier. She heard it straight from Mrs. Bedermeyer in the Headmistress's Office. Mrs. B. was there when . . . *she* toured the school. See?"

Oh, I saw, all right. Like twenty-twenty. Somehow these girls thought my mom was Aunt KiKi and Aunt KiKi was a real contessa.

"We heard that Mrs. B. wasn't quite sure she recognized your mom, until the stairs gave her away."

"Our source said the contessa sang almost the entire aria from *La Traviata* right there on the grand staircase."

The cucumber sandwich started giving me signals it was on the move again—and I wasn't sure which direction it was going. I crossed my fingers (and my legs) and hoped I was going to make it into one of those fifteen bathrooms at Fortier before something extremely embarrassing happened.

"I'm telling you, I'm just plain Isabella. Really. Not kidding."

"Wow." Oakleigh pushed her glasses up her nose. "That is so . . ."

"Real," Anisha said. "We didn't expect you to be . . ."

"Ordinary?"

"Ordinary. That's funny. I like you."

I was trying to smile, but the corners of my mouth had no plans turning in any direction but south.

"Isabella, we *totally* get that your mom doesn't want *anyone* here at school to know who you really are," Emory said. "But now that *we* know you are *you*, and you know that we know—"

"You still want to be our friend, right?" interrupted Oakleigh.

"*Best* friend," said Anisha.

Emory put her arm around my shoulders. "Don't worry, Isabella. We'll keep your secret."

Explore.

Create.

Imagine.

Stretch.

Be yourself.

Four out of five wasn't bad . . . was it?

11:52 a.m.
Scene 15/TAKE 1
Under the Dashboard of the Buick

I'm taking on the peculiar aroma of rubber mats mixed with cookie dough air freshener. All pretty awful when combined with how I already smell from stinky gym socks. I lift my head past the steering wheel and the view is uglier than I expected. And I'm not talking garbage cans or Nonni's shriveled tomato plants.

Frankie—*not* the cat—is knocking on our back door. Worse, way worse. If Frankie starts blabbing stuff he shouldn't be blabbing about, things could go "boom" even quicker than I thought.

Road trip is over.

Bye-bye, Buick.

11:55 a.m.
Scene 16/TAKE 1
On the Move

FYI, the row of bushes I climbed over through two backyards behind three garages is very, *very* prickly. (As in OUCH!)

Fingers part the curtains, and Auntie Ella's face peeks from the kitchen-door window. Her eyes widen and she smiles, sliding the deadbolt.

"Minnie! Look who is at our door here!"

I'm surprised either of them heard me knocking. Springsteen is wailing at a hundred decibels.

"Get in here, my sweetheart—fancy school girl—big star! What are you doing out there? Quick! Before those peeping Toms with cameras the size of bazookas come after you! They were click-click-clicking me when I took out the recycling, and I wasn't even wearing lipstick! It's Barnum and Bailey out there, only without elephants, although that one fella walking around in the gray sweat-suit comes close.

"*Madon,* look at your hair—going this way, that way. A brush or comb it needs, no? What's it doing outside? Snowflaking? In the middle of October? Or is Mrs. Findlay shaking her dust mop out the window again? MINNIE! TURN DOWN BRUCE! I KNOW THE MAN IS BORN TO RUN, BUT GIVE HIM A REST ALREADY! And *you,* Isabella, I'm kissing. Mmmmmwah. Mmmmwah. Ooo! Your cheeks are icebergs!"

I kiss Auntie Ella on both cheeks.

We're a two-cheek-kissing family. Anything less starts a family feud, and I'm already in enough trouble.

"Ooo! Ice cube lips, too." Auntie Ella fingers the sleeve of my T-shirt. "No wonder you're a Poopsicle! Wearing such a skimpy thing outside in this weather. You got nothing better? Or cleaner?" She sniffs. "You smell like furnisher wax, dirty socks, and Paulie Colandra's tires. What'sa matter? Washing machine not working over at your house?"

She grabs a long zebra-print sweater from the back of a kitchen chair and guides my arm through one sleeve.

"Warm up, *bambina*. And stop making with a frown face. We'll hide you from them pupserapsies, right, Minnie?"

"Paparazzi," says Aunt Minnie, shuffling in from the dining room, ballet flats on her feet.

"Pap? Pup? Pip? Who cares? *However*"—Ella reaches into the pocket of the zebra sweater and pulls out her phone—"you can give your old aunt one or two good pictures, right?" she says holding it close to my face. "Smile, Isabella. Show me some of that personality."

"Ella!" shouts Aunt Minnie as the light flashes.

"What?" she says with a shrug. "I'm not going to sell them to the rag sheets. Unless some big money is involved, of course." She gives a wink and stuffs the phone into the pouch of her leopard hoodie. "Isabella, what are you wearing on your legs there? Pajamas? Minnie, lunchtime and the kid is still wearing pajamas!"

"PJ pants," I tell her.

"Sweetie, you gotta talk into this good one," Ella says, pointing to her right ear. "I like the colors going on in that plaid. *Magenta* is what you call it. A pretty blue in there too."

Minnie frowns. "Turquoise, maybe aquamarine. It is not *blue*."

"Such a color expert," Ella says with a wave. Minnie turns her back and Ella sticks out her tongue. She looks at me and winks. "Maybe I'll get me a pair of those pink and *blue* PJs."

Minnie shakes her head. Her eyebrows furrow and her mouth shifts sideways as she takes slow baby-steps across the yellow and gray checked linoleum, nylon knee-highs rolled down around her ankles. Her bright pink tights are streaked with brown paint from the knees up, and she smells of turpentine, linseed oil, and garlic. She probably chopped more than a couple cloves for the sauce bubbling on the stove.

I sniff. "Something smells good."

"Of course it smells good," Ella says, walking over to the front burner. "Minnie's got everything in her Saturday gravy pot. Meatballs, sausage, spareribs, neck bones. The whole pig is in there swimming with the last of the summer tomatoes and basil from the garden."

Auntie Ella picks up the wooden spoon resting on the counter and gives the sauce a stir, then lowers the flame until it barely burns a light blue.

"You stay for rigatoni, Isabella," orders Minnie, one hand on her hip, the other pointing to the big stainless steel pot.

I notice the orange smudge across her chin. If it were on her sister, I'd say Auntie Ella was self-tanning again, but on Aunt Minnie I know the smudge is paint.

Every summer, way before I was born, the two of them visited Cousin Carmela on the family farm in Tuscany so Aunt Minnie could paint plein air. (Aunt Minnie told me that means painting outdoors.) Her arthritis is so bad now, she can no longer make the trip. Now instead of Italian landscapes, she paints portraits in the big room upstairs she calls her studio. It faces the backyard and has the best light in the house. Not the same as Italy, but Aunt Minnie says New Jersey light is all she's got.

She gave me the last landscape painting from her final

trip to Italy. A scene of my great-great-grandparents' farm in Pienza: green hills, swaying lavender, red poppies, tall deep green cypress trees, and way in the background, a white farmhouse. Her papa's. My Great-Great-Grandfather Giuseppe. Uncle Babe hung the painting over my bed. (It only took him three nails and one big hole in the plaster.) Mom even picked out a bedspread to match the purple flowers.

"Painting today, Aunt Minnie?" I say as we kiss.

"Little bit. Keeping my old fingers moving."

She smiles. So does Auntie Ella. That's when you can really see they are twins. When my aunts were younger, they looked identical. I've seen pictures in Nonni's photo albums, and you almost couldn't tell them apart. It's easy now because Minnie wears big white cat-eye glasses and her hair is red, like the hydrant down the street, while Ella's is the color of a Creamsicle. Neither has Nonni's cotton-candy beehive. Their hair is short, spiked, and gelled. Today, except for a fringe of short red bangs, most of Minnie's hair is under her favorite purple do-rag that she wears when she paints.

"Minnie. Look at our Isabella. Ammonia she's going to get, no?"

"New-moan-ya." Minnie rolls her eyes and claps her hands in prayer. "The woman refuses to listen to me."

Ella shrugs and hitches both thumbs inside the waistband of her bright green spandex biker shorts and gives them a hike. As she lifts her pants, spots on the leopard hoodie she's wearing start to jiggle. My grandmother is usually the designated checker when it comes to my aunt's undergarments. (As in: is Ella wearing any.) Pretty sure Grandma missed something important this morning.

My stomach growls.

"Minnie! The kid is hungry! Make this string bean something to eat."

"Of course I'll make something. What do you want, *cara mia*? I've got everything."

I move aside for Minnie to pull the refrigerator handle and peek over her shoulder as she opens the door.

Minnie slides her glasses down her nose, and squints. "Let's see what's in here. Bolognese from yesterday . . . veal involtini still good from Tuesday . . ."

Ella pokes me. "Eh. Pass on that. The veal is just okay."

"It's delicious, Isabella."

Ella whispers, "Oops. Thought that was her deaf side."

Minnie moves the containers from one shelf to the other. "I also have some eggplant."

"Minnie makes better than Constanza. Ravioli, too." Ella lowers her voice as if their older sister was able to hear two houses away. "Minnie's ravies are little pillows. Your great-grandmother's dough is tough, chewy—too much rolling and kneading. Of course, that's why her arms are in such good shape. Not as good as mine, though." Ella makes a muscle the size of a tangerine. "That's 'cause I do weightlifting. One pound. Each arm."

Minnie juts her chin toward the counter. "Look what's cooling on that rack next to the sink: *crostata di fichi e pere*—fig and pear tart. Carmela's recipe."

Ella nudges me in the ribs. "Remember when your Aunt KiKi was in that crazy *Search for Liars, Lovers*—whatever they called that show—and she asked the head writer to make her character have a craving for Carmela's crostata?"

"That show was garbage," says Minnie. "My pastry was the only good thing that happened on the program."

"I definitely want a slice of that," I say, already tasting the baked pears and Aunt Minnie's delicious crust.

"As much as you want. Take two. Three. You're a toothpick. Eat." Minnie pulls out the lunchmeat drawer. "Isabella, a sandwich maybe? Salami? Beautiful imported prosciutto de Parma? Or how about mortadella?"

Ella pokes me again with her elbow. "You know what your grandfather calls that, don't you?" she says with a laugh. "Bologna with Q-Tips."

"I'm so hungry I could eat a Q-Tip." I pat my stomach and smile. Grandpop would say coming over here was hitting the Daily Double: time to think *and* eat.

12:08 p.m.
Scene 19/TAKE 1

Ella grabs my arm and heads for the dining room. "Isabella, come while Minnie makes."

"Ella! Wait!" says Minnie before we reach the doorway. "Isabella, tie your aunt's shoelaces on those tugboats she calls sneakers before she trips and every bone in her body crumbles like a pignoli cookie."

"I can bend over and tie my own sneakers," Ella insists.

"I know you can bend over," says Minnie. "But nobody can get you back up."

I crouch and give Auntie Ella's purple laces a double tie while she tells me about bone density and her daily calcium intake: two cups of broccoli, one of kale.

"I'm what you call ax-toes untolerant. Can't drink milk no more. Doctor says eat green veggies like my younger Babe. These old bones are in good shape now, even though broccoli makes me gassy. Minnie, don't forget olives!" she yells over her shoulder, leading the way into the dining

72

room. She stops and whispers, "I like to suck on the salty black ones. I just have to remember not to swallow the pits."

Except for the bay window that faces Vincent's house next door, Aunt Minnie's paintings cover every inch of the four walls, floor to ceiling. I've never been to my great-great-grandfather's farm, but every time I'm in this room I feel like I'm standing in one of those fields in Italy. Aunt KiKi says it's *amahzzing* how Aunt Minnie can create a tree with only a few brushstrokes. Mom says a person can almost feel the Mediterranean breeze. I think she's right.

Directly across from the window is the sideboard that once belonged to my Great-Great-Grandmother Lucia back in Italy. Sitting on the marble top, front to back, end to end, are dozens of family photographs, like my grandparents' wedding portrait. (Grandpop's mustache was black and his sideburns were long and bushy.) There are pictures of Vincent blowing out his birthday candles when he was five, me sitting in a highchair with a bowl of spaghetti on my head, and one faded three-by-five of Uncle Babe in his plaid sport coat, back when he wasn't bald.

I like the photographs of Mom and her sisters at the Jersey Shore taken when they were little girls dressed in matching bathing suits, sitting on the sand under a striped umbrella, and another where the three of them are lined up in front of a cotton candy stand alongside my great-grandmother. (Aunt KiKi calls that snapshot "an example of the unsettling influence the Boardwalk had on Nonni's choice of coiffure.")

And way in the back where nobody can see, but I know it's there, is the only photograph I've ever seen of my parents. (Actually, it's three quarters of a photograph. Aunt Minnie cut part of my father's face out of the picture. But what's left looks handsome.)

"Come," Ella says, still leading me by the hand. "We're having a pic-a-nic."

"Pick-nick!" shouts Aunt Minnie from the kitchen.

12:13 p.m.
Scene 20/TAKE 1
Aunt Minnie and Auntie Ella's Living Room

"Older by two minutes," Ella mutters as she props a square pillow behind her back and squirms back and forth, getting comfortable on the beige couch. "A hundred and twenty seconds makes somebody so smart? Sit, my sweetheart."

She pats the cushion as I take a quick peek out the

window. I glance right, then left, look up the street as far as I can see, but there's no sign of Frankie or Vincent. The hot dog guy is still doing big business, though.

Ella gives the seat cushion another pat. "On my good side, so I can hear what you're saying. Otherwise all I see are lips moving—same as watching television with the sound off."

The living room smells of peppermint candies and Murphy Oil Soap, not counting Auntie Ella's Dolce & Gabbana. What she forgot with underwear, she made up in perfume. I was expecting the aroma of stale cigarette smoke, because even though Auntie Ella promised Mom she would quit we don't think she did. Either Auntie Ella has been forgetting where she hides her smokes, or Aunt Minnie opened the windows yesterday and aired out the room. That, however, would be unlikely, as the whole house is hermetically sealed the minute the temperature drops to sixty degrees.

The only room in the house where a window is unlocked and lifts up without a crowbar is one of the four in Aunt Minnie's studio. Grandma opens it a couple of times a week so she doesn't walk in one day and find Aunt Minnie passed out from turpentine fumes.

"Minnie! Hurry up in there," Ella calls, turning her

head toward the kitchen when she hears my stomach growl again. "We have a hungry girl! And warm up some of that eggplant left over from Wednesday!" Ella smiles. "Never get in trouble eating eggplant, right, Isabella?"

I nod and smile even though that is *so* not true.

Not true at all.

Seven Weeks Ago, Second Week of School
Founders Dining Hall, Fortier Academy
Sixth Grade Lunch

"Isabella, would you please pass the ketchup?" Emory asked, nodding to the bottle in the middle of our table next to a jar of mustard and stack of napkins.

"Sure. Hey, did you know back in 1933, one of these didn't even cost ten cents?"

"Huh?" She took the bottle from my hand and turned it upside down over her hot dog. "How do you know about *that*?"

"Uhhhhhhh . . ."

"*1933?*" she said, hitting the bottom with the heel of her palm.

(Uh-oh. I almost slipped into Isabella for real.) I hunched my shoulders and shrugged. "Read it *somewhere, I guess. I'm sort of good on . . . insignificant details.*"

"Well then promise me you'll be my study partner when history exams roll around. I hear through the grapevine Madame Bertrand loves to pack her tests with stuff just like that."

"Isabella can help *you* after she helps me," said Oakleigh, biting into the end of the bun.

(Me, a tutor? Who knew?)

"Uh . . . maybe we should eat!" I said, changing the conversation.

"What have you got in there?" Anisha asked as I opened the brown bag.

"Lunch. My Nonni packed my lunch again."

"What's a nonni? You mean *nanny*?"

"Of course she means *nanny*, don't you, Isabella?" said Emory.

"I haven't had a nanny since I was eight," Oakleigh said through a bite of hot dog, mustard smeared across her chin.

Emory swirled the end of a long french fry into the puddle of ketchup on her plate. "Isabella, are you talking about the woman who drives you to school every day in that cool vintage car? I thought you told us the other day she was your mom's personal assistant?"

"Her name is Rosie, right?" Oakleigh said, reaching for a napkin.

(I started thinking I might have to take notes. I had forgotten the little fib I'd told them about Aunt Rosalie.)

"Um. Yes. Rosie. That's right. She drives, cooks, and I guess what you call . . . nannies."

"She's a personal assistant, nanny, chauffeur, and a chef too?" Anisha asked, looking confused.

"Well . . . *kind of* . . . She sort of . . ."

"Multitasks?" said Oakleigh, wiping mustard off her chin.

"Exactly," I said with a long exhale. "Rosie multitasks . . . Let's eat!" I said in a second try at changing the topic.

I pulled the container from the soggy paper bag and Anisha leaned closer to my chair. "Is what's in there a favorite of . . . the *Contessa?*" she whispered.

"Well . . . uh . . . let's just say, I wouldn't be wrong if I told you that."

(Which was actually totally true. Aunt KiKi loved Nonni's eggplant.)

It was more than a week into school and I had given up trying to convince them I wasn't the daughter of a countess. The more I said I wasn't, the more all three believed I was. Yes, I knew this could turn into a big, ugly, soot-covered snowball growing bigger and bigger as it rolled down the drive at Fortier, but for right then, it just seemed like one harmless little fib.

Like Aunt KiKi said, *"Reality is nothing but perception, dahling. Go with the flow."*

So, I was . . . *flowing.*

Anisha peered into the container. "May I have a taste?"

"Me too?" chimed in Oakleigh.

"Make it three," said Emory, spoon already in her hand.

"Mmmm. This is delicious," Anisha said licking the back of her fork tines before passing the container on to Oakleigh, who eagerly dug in and helped herself to a generous serving.

"Yum," said Emory after getting her chance for a taste. "This eggplant parm is way better than anything my family gets from our take-out place."

I leaned back in the chair, folded my arms, and smiled. If there was one thing I knew about, it was eggplant. I grew up listening to Nonni rattle off the recipe a million times as she tried to teach Aunt Rosalie how to cook.

"See, the whole secret is cutting the eggplant *paper thin*. I'm talking transparent here. Then you dip the slices into some egg wash, followed by breadcrumbs—make sure you season that with lots of cheese and parsley, then sauté in small batches in extra virgin olive oil. Remember, don't have the oil too hot, or else you're gonna end up with a frying pan of black eggplant and a kitchen full of smoke. And don't even bother if you're not making your own marinara. Oh—important tip—whatever you do—no rubbery mozzarella like the pizza joints use. It's way better when you forget the moozt altogether and just go with Parmigiano-Reggiano all the way. The good stuff you grate yourself."

Oakleigh laughed. "Listen to you. You sound like a short-order cook."

Emory dropped her napkin on the table. "Big phony!"

My heart jumped into my throat, and that eggplant I had just swallowed felt like it was abruptly changing course and not far behind.

"Fffffffffff . . . ony?" I said as Emory looked in my direction with cold, narrowing eyes.

"Phony," she repeated.

Something told me that "snowball" was about to go splat.

I slowly lifted my butt off the chair and got ready to make a quick exit from Fortier—and back to Belleville. I just hoped Aunt KiKi was going to be able to get a refund on that big-bucks tuition check.

"Will you look at that big phony Jenna Colson sitting over there at the corner table. All smiles. Waving at the four of us, so sweet and friendly."

"Huh? Jenna Colson?" My rear end touched down with a soft landing on the seat of the chair and I took a breath, relieved it wasn't my name uttered through those gritted teeth.

"Wh-wh-why do you call her a phony, Emory?"

"Because, that girl is a person who pretends to be your friend, but it's all a big act."

"B-b-big . . . *act?*" I stuttered, my rear automatically lifting again off the chair.

"You have no idea, Isabella," said Oakleigh. "Jenna has spent every year at Fortier conning people into thinking she's a certain type of person when she's totally the opposite."

"But we've got her number," added Emory. "Those days of fooling us are over. We're not falling for that again."

"Wha-what did she do?" I said, reaching for my water bottle as my mouth began to feel like it was stuffed with cotton.

"What did she do? She pretended to help Anisha with a history project, but she was really after information to sabotage her during student council election!"

"We were both running for treasurer," Anisha said. "At the end of our debate she accused me of being dishonest! Me! As if I would *lie* about not returning a library book!"

"She was brutal. Turned the election upside down," said Oakleigh.

"I don't know why we were surprised," said Emory,

still glaring at the corner table. "Two years ago, she accused Sally Bernstein of using her sister Shani's math homework. That's how Jenna ended up winning fourth grade representative."

"She cornered me yesterday by my locker," Oakleigh said, looking over her shoulder and giving Jenna a little wave. "She told me she's running for Student Council *president* this year."

"Oh, great," groaned Emory, putting both elbows on the table and cupping her face in her hands.

Anisha turned to me and sighed. "Besides digging up dirt, Jenna also *influences* votes around here with candy."

"Candy?"

"Her parents own the biggest candy store in the city. Her mom supplies pink licorice, and Jenna sways the masses."

Oakleigh tapped her bottom teeth with one stem of her glasses, and looked up to the ceiling. "If only we could think of a way to beat her."

"To beat Jenna Colson," said Anisha, "you to have to be a person in this school with a clean slate and no baggage."

"That's it!" said Oakleigh.

"What's it?" asked Anisha.

"We put up a candidate who doesn't have baggage."

Anisha grinned. "I like it. We take away her ammunition. No bullets!"

"Okay, you two. I admit that sounds like a good idea," said Emory. "But who do we nominate?"

Oakleigh leaned back and folded her arms. "I don't know about you girls, but I'm thinking we have the perfect candidate sitting right here at this table."

"*Me?*" I said, spraying that last gulp of water across the table. "Whoa-whoa-whoa-wait a second!" I sputtered nervously. I grabbed napkins and mopped myself—and the tablecloth. "Me? *Me* is not a good idea."

"It's a great idea," said Emory. "You not only have a clean slate here at Fortier—it's totally blank. We can create an entire persona!"

I was pretty maxed out on "personas" right now. Not to mention what sort of deep sewer sludge I'd be falling into if anybody—especially Jenna Colson—found out about the real me. Living a double life was just a *little bit* juicier than an overdue library book.

"Don't worry," Emory whispered, leaning closer. "We won't give away your 'real' identity, of course."

"Of course not," assured Oakleigh.

"But . . . I don't have any experience being a class president. None. Zero."

"Who needs experience?" said Emory. "This is school, Isabella. On-the-job training. And you have the three best campaign managers: *un, deux, trois.*"

"Revenge against Jenna will be sweet," Anisha said with a broad smile. "Let her taste the fuzzy end of her own lollipops for a change."

Emory sighed. "It's too bad we can't tell everyone who you really are, Isabella."

"What?" My head jerked more than when Aunt Rosalie stops short at a red light.

"I'm just saying you'd win by a landslide if everyone knew you were royalty."

"Oh . . . yeah . . . royalty. But, uh . . . you promised not to blow my cover, remember? You won't put my picture in front of a castle in England or anything like that, right?"

"Castle? You have a castle? We thought your mother has a villa in Italy?"

"EMORY! Shhhhh!" said Anisha. "You weren't supposed to mention Italy!"

Oakleigh grabbed my arm. "Sorry, Isabella. We weren't being nosy—really we weren't. We were just being—"

"Curious," interrupted Anisha, finishing the sentence. "We Googled."

(I reminded myself to breathe.) "G-G-G-Googled?"

"Promise, you won't be angry—but we sort of . . .

well . . . *researched* your mom on my laptop. We typed in C – O – N – T – E – S – S —and before we hit the key for A, there she was—Contessa Francesca Monchetti."

The eggplant I had swallowed a while back finally reached my stomach, and I had the feeling it wasn't too happy being down there. In fact, it was giving all kinds of signs it was planning a quick exit. (And I wasn't too sure if the route was up . . . or down.)

"Egad, girl—her fashion salon in Milan is gorgeous!"

"And your New York penthouse with those windows overlooking Central Park is fabulous!" cooed Emory. "I love, love, love her black and white bedroom—I want to redecorate mine exactly like that—only with polka dots. And the pink living room is unbelievably awesome."

"Immensely awesome," agreed Anisha with a nod.

"I wish we had a silk couch in our living room," sighed Oakleigh. "Ours doesn't curve at all and it's boring brown washable suede. My mom says my little sister is going through a dangerous phase right now with peanut butter and jelly."

I didn't need the super brain of Jeffrey Levandowski to figure out they were describing the set on *Search for Truth, Lies and Love*. I knew every lavender pillow, pink vase, and silver-framed fake photograph in that entire make-believe apartment. I also didn't need Jeffrey to know that the website the girls were talking about was made by one of Aunt KiKi's "intensely devoted fans." Must have been a good one, too, because they all sounded like they believed that everything they saw and read on that site was real.

(My only hope right now was that they never got to the part where she time traveled. That one was difficult enough to explain to Nonni, but I was figuring impossible when it came to Emory, Oakleigh, and Anisha.)

Emory inched her chair closer to mine and held my hand. "Oh gosh, Isabella! How awful that your mother had no idea where you were for all those years and years."

"And the sad irony is you were living right in her own house, passed off as the housekeeper's grandchild!" Oakleigh said, teary-eyed.

Anisha gasped. "Oh lordy—was the housekeeper Rosie?"

Emory sighed. "It's all so *tragique*."

I gulped. (The "snowball" was running amok.)

"Um, this might be a good time to tell you about—"

"Your brother?" interrupted Oakleigh.

"Huh?"

"The website said his whereabouts were a mystery for years before you all were finally reunited."

"Oh. Right. My brother. Him. He . . . Him. Yes. It's complicated. *Very* complicated."

Anisha gave a sympathetic nod. "How utterly painful."

Actually, the search for her missing children was one of Aunt KiKi's favorite story lines. (Next to having amnesia. Twice.) She got to cry buckets and was nominated for her one and only Daytime Emmy.

"It's difficult to talk about, all right. In fact, a lot of it . . . I forget."

"Bad memories. We understand," she said, patting my hand.

Oakleigh nodded. "Especially since your father the secret government agent disappeared when you were born and has never been seen again."

Emory sighed. "*Si tragique!*"

"Dad?" I gulped. Whoa. Forgot all about that story line. "Uh, yeah, that was trajeek, all right. Very trajeek. I really can't talk about it . . . because, well, you know . . . top secret and all. Really and truly, I don't have any idea what happened to . . . Dad."

Which was the only absolute truth coming out of my mouth right now. I didn't know anything about my father, except for that half-torn photograph in Aunt Minnie's dining room. Nobody in my whole family, including

Mom, ever mentioned his name. Whenever I asked any questions about him, Mom would change the subject and give me a bowl of pistachio ice cream. Finally I stopped asking—and not just because I hate pistachio ice cream. Mom was eating my share and stretching out her hospital scrubs big-time.

"Is that why the contessa flies to Italy every weekend?" asked Emory. "Is your villa filled with happy memories?"

"Is it exquisitely beautiful?" Anisha asked. "What does it look like?"

"Um . . . look like?" My hands were sweating. Brain was racing.

"Yes, please, Isabella," agreed Emory. "Tell us all about it."

"Well . . . actually . . . it's sort of simple. More like *farmhouse*, really. Lots of rolling hills. Tall, dark green cypress trees. Poppies. Purple lavender."

Emory sighed. "Sounds like a painting."

"Uh. Yeah. Just like a painting."

12:25 p.m.
Scene 21/TAKE 1
Aunt Minnie and Auntie Ella's Living Room

"You listening to me, Isabella?"

"Huh? Oh, yes. Good playlist, Auntie Ella. I like that hip-hop you got on there."

"I hip *and* hop. Hey, Minnie!" Ella calls again from the couch. "Where are you? We're starving here! Our girl looks like she's going to faint!" She reaches over and strokes my hair. "I used to have brown hair like yours. I don't remember exactly when I had it, but I had it. At least I *think* I had it. Who knows how these roots started out? I've been bleaching since before Pearl Harbor."

Ella lifts the corner of my mouth with a push of her thumb. "Smile. Don't think about all that *tumulto* on the street. Noise. More noise. Police cars. News trucks. Hot dog trucks. That balloon guy—who's pretty good by the way. Probably a thief with what he's charging, but . . . eh. Let him make a few bucks, right?

"Everyone is crazy about those videos. I've seen the

91

episodes with me fifteen times already. Cosima, Mrs. Kostopoulos to you, called last night interrupting *Jeopardy!*—as if something is so important. She tells me she watched the videos on her son Bobby's flaptop. I could hear from her voice she's a sour pickle because her thirty-five-year-old son who does who-knows-what inside that garage down the street is not as talented as our Vincent."

"I saw her this morning from my bedroom window."

"Was she wearing those binoculars wrapped around her neck? Always with binoculars; bird watcher, she calls herself. Birds she's watching? Pfft. Hey, how about you and me watching that episode in the backyard under the big umbrella? 'The Contest,' Vincent calls it. Not a good title if you ask me. What contest? Who in this family has better legs than me? Minnie's ankles are cantaloupes. Some days they could be in a fruit stand. And anybody with one good eye, even poor half-blind Phil, your Poppi Two, rest in peace, knows my legs are better than Constanza's bony pins any day of the week.

"Our own mother said Constanza's knees were two alabaster doorknobs—*maniglie delle porte d'alabastro*—or something like that. I forget. Who can remember so long ago? And in Italian yet. We watch on my cell phone right here. See? I'm connected, sweetie. Got me a poker game on it too. Better than playing slots in Atlantic City like your grandfather. I don't lose money and don't lose time sitting on a bus that doesn't let you smoke for two and a half hours . . . *that is,* if I *still* smoked—which of course I do not."

She reaches into the pocket of her jiggling leopard hoodie and with the phone comes a crushed pack of Marlboro Lights.

"Auntie Ella!"

"Mother of Mercy! What are those things doing in there?" She makes her eyes all big and innocent and lifts her shoulders. "I'm shocked. Shocked, I tell you! See? This is my shocked face."

She opens her mouth wide and drops her jaw.

"Auntie Ella."

She puts a finger to her lips. "Don't worry. It's okay. I don't remember where I put the lighter, and Minnie doesn't keep matches in the house since I almost set fire to the wing chair." She pushes the pack in between the couch cushions. "I tell you, Isabella," she says, changing the subject, "when you say that funny line, I forget what it is, but it was funny . . . I almost you-know-what in my pants!"

"Ella!" says Minnie, walking slowly into the room holding a tray of sandwiches, a small platter of eggplant, and three glasses of Pellegrino.

"But—I *didn't*. Hear *that* in your good ear?"

"Never mind your pants. Or what you do in them. It's lunchtime. Eat your sandwich and eggplant. You too, Isabella. And remember, both of you, chew carefully. Don't choke."

"That's right. No choking like poor Arthur Schimlitz. For years I warned that man to stay clear of Rosalie's biscotti," Ella says, picking up her sandwich. "You just be careful swallowing, too, Isabella. We don't know the Heinie maneuver in this house."

Minnie looks to the ceiling and clasps her hands. "Give me strength."

I reach for my plate with the sandwich and olives and lift a wedge of eggplant from the platter with the pie server lying on the tray. I stare at the square of stacked breaded eggplant surrounded by a small pool of oozing marinara and bubbled Parmigiano-Reggiano crusted to a light brown. How could anything that delicious get somebody into so much trouble?

I sigh.

Not a big sigh.

Just a regular old ordinary sigh.

I cut into the eggplant layers, lift the fork, and open my mouth.

My eyes meet Aunt Minnie's, then Ella's.

I know that look.

It was the same one they both gave me when I was four and they caught me pocketing the quarter Nonni handed me for the offering basket at Sunday Mass.

Unfortunately, the sigh has them *thinking*.

I didn't plan either of them doing that.

12:31 p.m.
Scene 22/TAKE 1

"What's with all the sighing?" asks Auntie Ella, spitting an olive pit onto her plate.

"What?"

"Sighing. Like this: Aaaaaaaaaah," she says, mimicking me.

Minnie reaches over the coffee table and hands her sister a napkin. Ella wipes the roasted red pepper oil dribbling down her chin.

"What's the matter? You don't like the sandwich? Eggplant?"

"I love the sandwich." I take a bite and talk as I chew. "Delicious. Artichokes. Roasted pepper. Provolone. Mortadella. Yum. And eggplant, too. Love eggplant."

Minnie tears off a piece of roll. Her teeth are not as good as Ella's. "So? If everything is delicious, how come the sighing?"

I swallow. Clear my throat. Twice. "No reason. Just sighing, that's all. I guess I'm . . . *tired?*" I say, taking another bite. "But hungry! Mmm. Good sandwich. Good eggplant."

Minnie nods to her sister. "Hear her, Ella? Good sandwich, she says. Good eggplant."

Ella leans her elbow on the arm of the couch and starts tapping her chin with her finger. "Uh-huh. I'm looking how you are looking and hearing what I am hearing. I'm putting three and three together . . ."

"Something is fishy—and I'm not talking anchovies."

Minnie puts her napkin on her lap. "What's the matter, Isabella?"

I take two bites of sandwich. Another two. One more. Then I stuff my mouth with three forks of eggplant. "Nofphing," I say, resembling a blowfish.

Ella sucks the life out of another olive pit and then pouches it in her left cheek. "Well, something happened. You're not keeping no secrets, are you?"

"Secrets?" I say with a big swallow. "Why would you think that? Gee, all these questions. I'm feeling like I'm on *Law and Order* or something."

Ella licks her fingers. "We only watch *Law*. We fall asleep before *Order*."

"Ella thinks she's watching your cousin Anthony. He's a third cousin on your Poppi Natale's side of the family." Minnie sips her Pellegrino. "He's the detective. Works not far from your fancy school up on that hill."

Ella pops another olive into her mouth. Where the first pit went is anybody's guess, because it's not on her plate. Her lips pucker as she starts sucking again.

"I never knew I had a cousin who's a detective. Did he ever, oh, you know, put a person in *jail* for . . . fibbing?"

Minnie stares at me. "You mean *lying?*"

Ella spits out two pits. "That's fraud! I know my law. Or wait a minute—is that order? Penalty is one to three in the slammer. Unless you're a big-time lying, faking imposter, then you're headed up the lazy river for a ver-yyyyyyy long time. Like Carlo, your third cousin once removed, the one with the hairy knuckles. For years Constanza told everybody he was in college at Trenton State."

Minnie dabs the corner of her mouth with her napkin. "Your great-grandmother, what a storyteller. The man didn't 'graduate' for twelve years."

Ella laughs. "His varsity sweater was striped."

Minnie nods. "That man inherited bad genes from who knows where in the family."

I look down and check my hands.

Do I see a hair on my left pinky?

"Uh, I think I have to go now. I have to call my mother. Or she has to call me. Or, actually . . . I think I hear her. Uh-huh. Yup. That's her calling me, all right. I better go. Thanks for lunch, Aunt Minnie."

I put my plate with the half-eaten sandwich on the end table and spring from the couch.

Minnie stands too.

She puts her hands on her hips and stiffens her back, which is not easy for her to do. She's giving me a look like ice cream wouldn't melt in her mouth. (Even Holsten's.)

"Is-a-bel-lah Fil-o-me-na."

Two names and eight syllables: That many syllables are never a good sign. Especially when the face of the person saying them is turning the same color as her hair. I slowly lower my rear end back down onto the couch.

"You sit down too, Aunt Minnie. Relax."

"Never mind, me relaxing. What's going on?"

"Don't get excited," I say calmly, hoping Auntie Ella remembers where Minnie keeps her high blood pressure medicine.

"I'm not EXCITED!" she says, even though her eyes are now bulging and what's left of her sparse eyebrows have gone up so high, they have disappeared somewhere under her bangs. "See? I am now sitting and listening to what you are going to tell me even though my carotid artery is pulsing out of my neck."

That was not an exaggeration. I see a blue vein throbbing from where I'm sitting on the couch.

"Okay, okay. But promise not to tell Mom or Nonni."

Ella looks at Minnie. "Uh-oh. Here comes a good one."

"Well, see, it all started as a simple misunderstanding. It could have happened to anybody. Really. A person eats a cucumber sandwich with no crust, drinks something named Earl, and before she knows it, she's saying stuff she shouldn't be saying and people are believing stuff they shouldn't believe, and there you have it. You understand what I'm saying, don't you?"

Minnie crumples her napkin in her fist. "No."

"No?"

Minnie pushes her glasses down her nose and leans forward. "Ella, do you know what she's talking about?"

Auntie Ella licks marinara sauce off her thumb. "I know cucumbers don't agree with me, either. They make enough gas to fill the tank on Rosalie's Buick."

Minnie leans back in her chair and rubs her temples with both hands. "I'm getting a headache, and have agita from both of you. Spill whatever you need to spill already. And I'm not talking Pellegrino."

"*Maybe* I should call Jeffrey."

"Jeffrey?" Aunt Minnie scowls. "What does he have to do with this?"

"Not that much, but he's better at explaining things than I am."

"Wait a minute! Is he the fibber?" Ella says, making her shocked face again.

"Not exactly. He's more the *helper* to the fibber. Jeffrey is very organized and excellent at keeping track of complications. You'd be surprised how a few little fibs can get very confusing. It's not easy living a double life. It really isn't. Especially when you're running for class president."

Now it was Aunt Minnie's turn to make the shocked face.

Auntie Ella reaches into her pocket. "I'm texting that kid to get over here right now."

"*You* text Jeffrey?" I ask.

"After Vincent and Cheng's Chinese Take-Out, he's number three on my contacts list."

100

Jeffrey squirms in the flowered wing chair with the singed cushion, nervously rolling and unrolling the cuffs on his checked shirt. "Uhhhh . . ." he says, looking up to each corner of the ceiling, chewing on his lower lip. "Should I start from the beginning?"

Aunt Minnie sucks in her cheeks. "Beginning is good."

"Actually," Jeffrey says meekly, turning toward me, "I wasn't there at the *beginning* beginning. I came in at the second part of the beginning. Or was it the third part of the beginning?"

"Third. *I* wasn't even at the first. It was Mrs. Bedermeyer who started it."

Ella looks at Minnie. "Who is Mrs. Bederwhatsits?"

"She's the secretary to Madame Bonier, the headmistress at the academy," I explain. "While taking a tour of the school back last summer, Aunt KiKi somehow found her way to the grand staircase and began singing an aria from *La Traviata*. That's how Mrs. Bedermeyer recognized her as the Contessa from *Search for Truth, Lies and Love*."

Minnie leans back in her chair and looks to the ceiling. "Again with those steps."

"Aunt KiKi asked Mrs. Bedermeyer to keep her identity

a secret, but Mrs. Bedermeyer didn't. She told someone 'the Contessa' had enrolled a new student. Then that person told another person, who told somebody else, and—

"Telephone!" cries Auntie Ella.

Aunt Minnie raises an eyebrow at Ella.

"What?" Ella says with a shrug, popping another olive into her mouth. "You never played that game before?"

"She's right, Aunt Minnie. It was just like telephone. That's why the facts got all mixed up!"

"Exactly," interrupts Jeffrey. "By the time the rumor got to Isabella's friends, the story turned into Isabella being the daughter of an Italian countess. Then the girls Googled 'The Contessa' and found some crazy fan site that made it seem like KiKi's plot line from the soap opera wasn't fiction, but the truth."

"I tried to convince them I wasn't who they thought I was, but nobody would believe me. After a while . . . I just went along with it."

"You 'embraced' it!" said Ella, spitting a pit onto her plate.

Minnie gives Ella another hard stare, then rolls her eyes to the ceiling and sighs. "Anything else, Isabella?"

"Well . . ." I turn to Jeffrey.

"The biggest mess is from those videos going viral. Now Isabella and her real life are all over TV and her friends from Fortier probably think she's a fibbing, faking, phony."

"Outed," Minnie says.

"Fraud!" Ella says with a decisive nod. "Just like your second cousin Carlo!"

"I know I'm an old lady, and *nobody* ever wants to listen to me—"

"Are you looking at *me?*" interrupts Ella.

"Yes, I'm looking at *you*. And now I'm looking at Isabella. *Ciò che una contorta storia!*"

Jeffrey looks at me. "What does that mean?"

"I don't know, but I'm pretty sure it isn't 'whoopee.'"

Minnie frowns. "Isabella, why did you pretend to be somebody else?"

I lean back on the couch and sigh. "I don't know . . . the gargoyles made me do it?"

Minnie shakes her head and sighs. "A comedian like her grandfather, this one."

Ella pouches the olive pit in one cheek. "Minnie doesn't think that's funny, Isabella. I know because I've seen the face for the last ninety-one years."

"I guess I was afraid I wouldn't fit in at my new school, Aunt Minnie," I answer softly as I hang my head.

Jeffrey—a smart boy like you, and you let your best friend carry on with that ridiculous charade?"

Ella coughs and spits another pit. "I like playing charades too!" She taps two fingers on her forearm. "First word—second syllable."

Minnie rolls her eyes and I turn to the wing chair. "Go ahead, Jeffrey. Tell Aunt Minnie."

"Uh . . . well, I did. I told Isabella to come clean about everything. And she was going to tell the truth. She was . . . but . . ."

Aunt Minnie impatiently drums her fingers on the arm of the chair. "But?"

Jeffrey gulps. "I sort of made things more complicated."

"WAIT!" Ella shouts, holding up her hand. "Is this intermission? Sounds like we're getting to another good part, and before we get there, I want to microwave some popcorn." She claps her hands. "Hey! Who's up for Orson Rodentbacker?"

Seven Weeks Ago
That Particular Saturday Afternoon . . .
The Mall

Jeffrey and I went to the mall with his mom. It's the very fancy mall that doesn't even have a food court, but that's okay because it has big soft leather chairs where people can sit and watch other people, which is what Jeffrey and I like to do because we don't have money to buy anything anyway.

Jeffrey and I were sitting in the comfortable chairs in the center of the mall while his mother shopped for shoes in Bloomingdales.

(My mom does *not* buy shoes there. I don't know much about dating, but I keep telling her that if she wore better-looking shoes and something besides baggy nurses' scrubs, maybe she wouldn't be spending every Saturday night with Grandma and Nonni playing Bingo in the church cafeteria. But I'm only eleven, so what do I know?)

Jeffrey tore off a piece of the pretzel we were sharing and handed me the rest. "Want to play handkerchief, Kleenex, or sleeve?"

That's a game we made up sitting on the curb in front of our houses the summer we were six. We looked at people walking down the sidewalk and called out if they used a handkerchief, Kleenex, or their sleeve. In our neighborhood, sleeve was mostly the winner.

"Sure," I said, chewing a piece of soft pretzel. "Your mom's probably trying on tons of shoes. We have lots of time."

"Me first," said Jeffrey. "Coming toward us: The lady pushing a stroller. Kleenex."

"Man in suit. Handkerchief."

"Sneaker guy. Sleeve. You're going to tell your new friends the truth, right?"

"Definitely sleeve. Good one. Of course I'm going to tell them the truth . . . eventually."

"Bald guy to your right—Kleenex. Not eventually, Isabella. Soon!"

"Lady with glasses and weird hat. Kleenex. Yes, after the election."

"Not *after* the election. Lady in shades: handkerchief. With monogram."

"Wow. Excellent. Gray-haired lady to your left: handkerchief. Telling them is harder than you think, Jeffrey. They really like me—or like *that* Isabella, anyway. I'm kind of popular at this new school."

"What are you talking about? You're not even you! On the left. Mother with three kids: tissue."

"I'm the me they think I am. And like KiKi says, '*reality is only perception.*'"

"Aunt KiKi?" Jeffrey rolled his eyes. "You're quoting *Aunt KiKi?* Let me refresh your memory, Isabella. Your aunt was the woman who broke into song on that staircase at Fortier Academy and started this whole snowball rolling."

"I know, I know. But I can't tell them about me *just yet.* The girls are counting on me to win the election and beat Jenna Colson. I told you about her, remember?"

"Yeah, I remember. Guy in cowboy boots: sleeve? Jenna isn't a good excuse, Isabella. You have to tell your friends the truth. Promise me you will."

"All right already. Nag nag. I promise. I'll tell them. Next week."

"This week."

"Okay, *this* week. Wednesday. Or Thursday. Maybe Friday."

"Isabella!"

"Tuesday! I'll tell them Tuesday."

Jeffrey was just about to make me do our secret handshake (minus the spitting, of course, since we were at the mall), when we heard my name being called out from somewhere.

"Hey! ISABELLA!"

I turned behind me to see Emory and Oakleigh waving, and walking toward us. Jeffrey leaned across the fat arm of the maroon leather chair. "Are those girls the girls I think they are? Wow."

"What do you mean, *wow*?"

"Just, you know . . . wow, that's all."

"Hi, Isabella!" said Emory.

"Hey! Emory! Hi, Oakleigh," I said, getting off the chair.

"We almost didn't recognize you, Isabella, in your civilian clothes," said Emory with a hug.

"Oh, right. These old things," I said brushing pretzel crumbs off my khaki shorts and Sisters of Mercy green sweater. "This sweater is from ages ago."

"Isabella, I can't believe you're *here*."

"In the mall?"

"In New Jersey."

Emory leaned close to my ear and whispered, "We thought you spent every weekend you-know-where with you-know-who."

"Gosh, Isabella, if we had known you were here for the weekend, we could have all come to the mall together."

"Yeah. Right. I should have thought of that. But, um, coming here was kind of . . ."

"Unplanned," interjected Jeffrey. "Spontaneous. No planning involved."

"Yes. That's right. No planning involved."

Oakleigh looked at him and smiled. "Thank you for clarifying," she said, curling a strand of her dark hair around her finger. "So, um, Isabella . . . who's your friend?"

"My friend?" Jeffrey jabbed my side with his elbow. "Ow—oh—*him?* You mean this person here? This is Jeffrey."

"Hi. I'm Oakleigh."

"I'm Jeffrey."

"I just told her that," I said under my breath.

Jeffrey looked at me. "I heard you." Then he looked at Oakleigh. And smiled. (Ever since he got his braces removed, he used any excuse to show off his straight teeth.) "I like your glasses, Oakleigh."

"I like yours too, Jeffrey."

Jeffrey turned to me. "See? Oakleigh and I have something in common."

I rolled my eyes.

"So, Isabella, what are you doing in the mall with *Jeffrey*?" Oakleigh asked.

"Doing? Oh . . . uh . . . What *are* we doing, Jeffrey?"

"You mean what are we doing *here?*" he answered, as he tried to make himself taller than Oakleigh. (Which, wasn't working.)

"Yes. What are we doing here and why are we together?"

He looked at me and stammered, "Well, uh, you see my . . . my . . . aunt . . . *Rosie* . . ."

I gave a whiplash turn. "*Your* Aunt Rosie?"

"The Contessa's assistant?" said Emory.

"Uhhhhhh. Yes. Her. See . . . Rosie, who is my *aunt,* came to visit my *mom,* who is her *sister,* younger sister—a lot younger sister, and Isabella came with Rosie to visit *me* and *we* came along with my mom to the mall to just . . . you know . . . hang out while she's buying shoes."

"That's right. We're just hanging out," I said, nodding. "Because, like Jeffrey said, we're friends."

"Not boyfriend, girlfriend friends," said Jeffrey, still smiling at Oakleigh. "Just *friends.*"

"Brainstorm," squealed Emory. "Isabella, if Jeffrey's aunt drives in from New York next weekend to visit her sister and your you-know-who is flying you-know-where, you could come home with me Friday and Oakleigh, Anisha, and both of us can work on our campaign."

"Great idea, Em," agreed Oakleigh. "We really should spend a whole weekend mapping out strategy. Don't forget, we're going to war against Jenna's candy with your eggplant parmigiana, Isabella. Maybe you whip up a batch over at Emory's to freeze for the rally."

Jeffrey turned to me. "You know how to make eggplant parm?"

"*Yes*, Jeffrey," I said through a gritted smile. "Of course I know how to make eggplant parm. You know that."

"Oh. *Right*. Yeah. Sure. I know that."

Emory reached into her bag and took out a tube of light pink lip-gloss. "Let's plan for Friday night."

"Maybe Rosie can drop Jeffrey off at Emory's on Saturday and we could all go to a movie or something together," said Oakleigh.

"Yeah! That sounds gr—"

"Mmmmmmm?" (My turn for the stealth elbow jab.) "I think Jeffrey is busy, aren't you, Jeff?"

"I am?" he said, rubbing his side as I shot him a hard stare. "I mean, I am."

"Oh well, another time, I guess," said a disappointed Oakleigh.

Emory dropped the gloss back into the bottom of her bag. "Oops, look at the time. We better head out, Oak.

My dad is picking us up at four by the Neiman entrance. Remember Isabella: Sleepover and election strategy at my house."

"And eggplant!" said Oakleigh. "Hope to see you again, Jeffrey."

I watched as Jeffrey waved goodbye to Oakleigh until she and Emory disappeared around the corner by Pottery Barn.

"Excuse me," I said, grabbing him by the arm, "but I thought you wanted me to tell the truth. How am I going to that sleepover at Emory's house without my mother wanting to first talk to her parents?"

"Sorry. My bad. I don't know what I was thinking."

"You were thinking about Oakleigh, is what you were thinking."

"Oakleigh?"

"I saw the way you looking at her."

"I wasn't looking at her."

"Uh-huh."

"If I was looking at Oakleigh, then you look at Frankie Domenico."

"Jeffrey Levandowski! I cannot believe those words came out of your braces-free mouth. You deserve Palmolive for that one. And just how do you suppose I'm going to tell those girls the truth now, after your addition to my story? They'll think I'm a even bigger fibber than before."

"You graduated to lying all by yourself before today."

"Well, you've helped it along."

I sat back down on the leather seat cushion and leaned my head on the smooth, fat arm. "And now I have to make eggplant, too!"

"*You* started this, not me."

"Yeah, but I was going to take your advice and get out of it. Now you've made that impossible. I'm ruined. Dead meat. Toast."

"Wait a second." Jeffrey snapped his fingers. "Stop groaning. I've got an idea. I think we can do this."

"*We?*"

"Follow me. See that fancy stationery store four down on the left?"

Stationery store?

"Well?" he called over his shoulder, running ahead. "Are you coming or not?"

I had no idea what was in Jeffrey's head, but I knew from experience, the boy had his moments. Besides, being a genius on the computer, it was because of Jeffrey we made all that money by letting kids get stuck and unstuck on Nonni's plastic slipcovers. I figured one hundred thirty-six dollars and eighty cents at least deserved the respect of following him into a card store.

"Listen," he said in a low voice as we stood huddled next to each other in front of skirted table stacked with boxes of note cards. "Emory's parents think your mother is the Contessa, and a very private person, correct?"

"Correct. So?"

"So her parents will totally understand if your mom, 'the Contessa,' doesn't call them *personally*, and thank them for having you over to their house."

"They will? Why?"

"Because she writes them a thank-you note on one of her fancy 'C' for Contessa *note cards*. Get what I'm saying? But it's your *real* mom, Corinne, who writes the note on the 'C' stationery that *you* give her as a *gift* today."

"So I buy one of these," I say, tapping a pile. "How am I going to convince my mom to write a note instead of meeting Emory's parents? Or phoning? Or not signing her own name on the note? What about all that?"

"Your lack of faith deeply hurts me, Isabella. Don't you think I already thought of that? *You* are going to tell your mom that writing a note to other parents is the way it's done at Fortier Academy. You ask her to sign her name using only her initial C, because . . ."

"Go on."

"I haven't quite figured that out yet."

"Well, I'd say that's the most important part, Jeffrey."

"Hey, you're the one with the big imagination around here. You think of something."

I chewed on my thumbnail and thought. "I don't know . . . What about signing one letter is more French? How's that?"

"Sounds good to me."

"I suppose if she resists, I could beg a little, too. I'm not too bad at that. I convinced Nonni to keep a cat in the house, so convincing my mother to do this should be a piece of cake."

I picked up a small package of note cards. "Here's one with a gold C. Embossed, too." I smiled at Jeffrey. "I think this idea might just work."

I look at Aunt Minnie.

"If it wasn't for Vincent's videos, I think I could have pulled off this double-life thing right through twelfth grade. Mom hardly ever had time to go to my parent-teacher conferences at Merciful Sisters—and that school is only down the street. I think I really could have gone seven years without her ever showing up at Fortier. It could have worked."

"Except for the eggplant," Jeffrey says.

I nod. "I don't know how many times I could have come up with a good enough reason to convince Nonni to make more pans of eggplant. She was suspicious with the story I gave for the first batch."

Ella sucks salt off her fingers and shakes her head. "I am disappointed in you, Isabella. Very disappointed. Extremely disappointed. Minnie!" she says, slapping the arm of the sofa. "Are you hearing what our great-grandniece just told us? Can you believe it? Traitor! . . . She used Constanza's eggplant recipe instead of yours!"

Aunt Minnie looks up to the ceiling and sighs. "I need a sip of limoncello."

"I need more popcorn!"

"I need to go to the bathroom." I shoot a quick glance in Jeffrey's direction and lift my chin toward the stairs. "Bathroom? Jeffrey? *Bathroom.*"

"Bathroom?"

"You know. Upstairs," I say, signaling with a nod to the floor above.

"Oh! 'Upstairs.' Right . . . I think I have to go to the bathroom too."

Minnie folds her arms. "You go to the bathroom *together?*"

"No-no, not *together* together. I wait for Jeffrey. Jeffrey waits for me."

"Or I wait for Isabella. She waits for me."

"I really, *really* have to go," I say, bolting from the couch and running for the stairs.

"Me too," Jeffrey says, following so close behind that he bumps into me.

"I don't want you two wasting time up there," orders Minnie when we are already halfway up the stairs. "I'm ninety-one and not getting any younger. I want all the facts before going to the grave, so make it snappy."

1:03 p.m.
Scene 25/TAKE 1
Aunt Minnie and Auntie Ella's Upstairs Hallway

Jeffrey walks past me heading for the bathroom, and I grab him by his checked shirttails.

"You want to go first?" he whispers.

"*No,* I don't want to go first. Or second. I don't have to use the bathroom."

"You don't?"

"Coming up here was an excuse so we could talk. Plan our next move."

"What move?"

"How to get out of here and figure out what I'm going to say to Emory, Oakleigh, and Anisha before Nonni gets a hold of me and I'm swallowing soapsuds—that move."

"But . . ."

"But *what?*"

"I really *do* have to go to the bathroom," Jeffrey says, crossing his ankles.

I sigh. "Oh, sweet ravioli."

I hear a flush . . . squeaking faucets . . . and running water with way too much splashing in the sink.

Jeffrey opens the door, steps back into the hall, and I grab his arm.

"Okay, Levandowski, exactly *what* have you been up to?"

"Huh?" he says, scratching his head. "What do you mean, what have I been up to? I peed."

"I know you did *that*. Why have you been texting Auntie Ella?"

"Oh, that. I sold her wrapping paper from my school's fundraiser. I update her on the order. She's my best customer. She bought seventy-five dollars' worth of merchandise: two rolls of red, one of—"

"I don't want to hear about wrapping paper!"

"Want to hear about Emory, Oakleigh, and Anisha driving me crazy with the texts they've been sending since last night?"

"They texted you?"

"See for yourself." Jeffrey takes the phone from his back jeans pocket. "First one is from Oakleigh. 'OMG.

IzzB on TV? UGTBK!!!!' That means 'You've got to be kid-ding.'"

"I know what it means."

"*Somebody* is cranky." He hands over the phone. "There are at least fifty from Oakleigh saying, 'CALL ME'—cap letters—followed by a row of exclamation points. Three more dozen saying 'CMON!!!!!!!' Oh, and this one from Emory—'R.I.Diculous.'"

"Do you think that means R.I.Diculous bad, or R.I.Diculous good?"

Jeffrey rolls his eyes. *"Seriously?"*

"So you're saying they've seen the videos?"

"Dude. You're really asking me that? Yes, there is more than an excellent mathematical probability that Emory, Oakleigh, and Anisha are three of the eleven million peo-ple who have seen those videos."

I quickly scroll through the messages. "Did they say they hate me?"

"Didn't see, but wouldn't blame them. You told some whoppers, Izzie. Oh, and you might want to take a look at that text from Frankie."

I grit my teeth. "Domenico."

"Well, what did you expect from Domenico? You never saw that coming?"

"Well, what did you expect from him? Come on, it's Frankie. You never saw that one coming?"

"I should have seen that one, all right. Especially after what happened at Holsten's two weeks ago. The girls had all been inviting me to their homes, so I knew the polite thing to do was invite them to my house too. But since there was no way I could bring them to a penthouse apartment that only existed on the set of *Search for Truth, Lies and Love,* and sitting next to a hissing furnace in Belleville while listening to my grandparents argue about spoons might have been just a *little* difficult to explain, I took them all to Holsten's.

I had an open tab thanks to my deal with Vincent, so I treated. And because Marie, who's been a waitress there forever, always treats me like royalty, I figured going there was a no-brainer.

My luck that Domenico would be showing his face at Holsten's the same day I was there with Emory, Oakleigh, and Anisha.

Everything was working out fine until Frankie strolled in and plopped his rear end down on the booth behind us. The big eavesdropper heard stuff he shouldn't have heard—but did.

"You should have never picked up his tab, Isabella," Jeffrey said, shaking his head.

"I should have unless I wanted him to blab the truth about me right then and there in front of Emory, Oakleigh, and Anisha."

"ISABELLA! We're getting closer to ninety-two down here! Get down here— and make it snappy!"

"Be right there, Aunt Minnie." I turn to Jeffrey. "Listen, when you were in there doing what you were doing, I came up with an idea. Suppose—just suppose . . . I blame everything that happened on my evil twin sister."

Jeffrey stares at me. *"Evil twin?"*

"Who took over my identity."

"Evil twin?"

"It worked on *Search for Truth, Lies and Love.* Twice. I even remember some of the dialogue. I can do it! I'll tell them my *very* twisted twin sister, Gabriella—that's a good name, right? Yeah, Gabriella escaped from one of those 'asylums.' I was kidnapped and she's been holding me hostage while pretending to be me since the day of the tea."

"Isabella, are you hearing yourself?"

"The twin thing isn't working for you, huh? What about amnesia?"

"Isabella."

"Amnesia always works."

"Isabella."

"Jeffrey, I can't have my new friends think I'm a fibber, faker, and phony!"

"Yeah, well, that's a tough one, because you *are* a fibber, faker, and phony."

"ISABELLA!" shouts Aunt Minnie from the living room. "You two get yourselves downstairs this minute."

"We better go, Isabella," Jeffrey says, turning me toward the stairs. "You aunt sounds like she's going to burst a corpuscle."

"Wait. Wait! Wait a minute!" I snap my fingers. "I've got another idea."

"Like your last one? Forget it. Let's go," he says with another nudge.

"Just hear me out . . . Look, the whole mess spun out of control because of the worship website to the Contessa, right?"

"So?"

"So, if the website got me in, maybe the website can get me out. At least buy me some time until Tuesday and the election against Jenna."

"And how is *that* going to happen?"

"I convince the girls it's not me that's fake—it's those videos!"

"Hold it! Rewind, Antonelli. True is fake and what is fake is true?"

"Good idea, right?"

"Excuse me, but there are eleven million people who have seen *you* as you!"

"But I only have to convince *three* of them it's the videos that are pretend." I smile at Jeffrey. "With your help, of course."

1:09 p.m.
Scene 27/TAKE 1

"ISABELLA and JEFFREY! Don't make these arthritic feet climb those stairs and come after you! Hurry up!"

"But don't slide on the bannister," shouts Auntie Ella. "I was seeing stars when I hit the newel post after taking that shortcut myself last week."

Jeffrey looks at me. "Ouch."

"Never mind Auntie Ella. You'll help me, right?"

"Me?"

"Well, you don't think I'm going to ask Frankie, do you?"

Jeffrey folds his arms and sighs. "Okay. So what do I have to do?"

"No big deal. Just hack into the worship website."

"*What?*"

"Can't do it?"

"Of course I can do it, but—"

"Great! Get into the site and send an IM to the web-master saying the Contessa wants to talk. A devoted fan won't refuse an offer like that. We get a phone number, then I call doing my imitation of Aunt KiKi and ask for a personal *favor*. Something like this: *Please include the name of my long-lost daughter, Isabella, on your fabulous site, dahling. It would make me immensely happy! And I would be eternally grateful if you add that she is a young actress working incognito.*"

"Incognito?"

"Undercover, Jeffrey. Undercover . . . *She's involved with making mockumentary films in New Jersey with her brother, the talented Vincent Palumbo.*"

Jeffrey shakes his head. "Are you kidding? You're an actress making a movie? That's the best you can come up with?"

"You didn't like evil twin, and yes, in less than five minutes, that's the best I can come up with. Why can't it work? Vincent said I sound just like Aunt KiKi. *Sort of.* Anyway, once the new info is on the website, you convince Oakleigh to look at it, she'll read it, tell Emory and Anisha, and then they'll think what's on those videos with me being the real me is not the real me but me acting the part for a movie. I have to make them believe I'm still the

Contessa's daughter, who is an actress making a film in New Jersey with her brother. At least until after the election on Tuesday. They're counting on me to beat Jenna, and once that happens, I'll confess everything and come clean."

"Really?" Jeffrey's brows furrow low behind his glasses and he squints as he stares into my face. "You promise?"

I nod. "Promise. Cross my heart. So . . . are going help me?" He sighs. I sigh. "Great! Now all we have to do is get to a computer." I snap my fingers. "Your house!"

The kitchen door slams.

"IS-A-BELL-AH! Are you here?"

"Oh no! Vincent! He found me! I hear him coming through the kitchen!"

"ISABELLA!" Ella calls. "Pupserapsies and that cutie-patootie Frankie are on the porch here banging at the front door!"

"ISABELLA!" Vincent shouts, now tramping through the dining room. "The reporter is next door at my house waiting for you! ISABELLAAAAAAHHHHHH!"

I grab Jeffrey's hand. "We gotta get out of here!"

"Out *where?*" Jeffrey says with a look of panic on his face. "We're on the second floor!"

"This way!" I say, pulling him into Aunt Minnie's studio. I spin around the room and point. "Open one of these windows!"

"Did you not hear me, Isabella? We're two floors up!"

"Stop talking and help me open this," I say, pushing my shoulder into the window, which won't budge.

"Whoa!" Jeffrey stands frozen in the middle of the room, staring at the row of canvases on the far wall. "Do you know Aunt Minnie is painting people who aren't wearing their clothes? Double WHOA! Is that one in the corner . . . *Auntie Ella?*"

"Bingo!" I say, lifting the third window with my first try.

"Out. Now! You first!" I say, giving him a push.

"Isabella," he cries, straddling the windowsill, eyes like saucers as he looks down. "We are on the SECOND FLOOR!"

"Stop worrying. See the trellis? It's like a ladder—only with ivy. It's been done. Trust me."

OW! YOUR FOOT IS ON MY FACE!

THEN MOVE YOUR FACE! MY FEET ARE COMING DOWN WHETHER THERE'S A FACE UNDER THEM OR NOT!

HEAD FOR THE BACKYARD.

WATCH OUT FOR THE. . .

OWWWW!

FORSYTHIA BUSHES.

THANKS.

NOT THAT WAY! WE CAN'T GO TO YOUR HOUSE NOW! THAT'S THE FIRST PLACE VINCENT WILL LOOK!

THEN WHERE? WE HAVE TO GET TO A COMPUTER!

I HAVE MY ID CARD! WE CAN USE A COMPUTER AT FORTIER.

WE'LL CUT OVER TO GARRABRANT, MAKE OUR WAY TO WATCHUNG, THEN UP TO SCHOOL.

WE'RE WALKING ALL THE WAY UP THERE?

RUNNING.

RUNNING?!

IT'S FOUR MILES!

FINE. WE'LL BIKE IT.

WE DON'T HAVE BIKES!

JOEY PICCOLO AND HIS BROTHER HAVE BIKES. THEIR GARAGE IS ALWAYS UNLOCKED.

WE'LL "BORROW" THEM.

WE'RE STEALING NOW?

RUMFF?

WOOF! WOOF! WOOF! WOOF!

FORGET THE BIKES! HERE COMES BOOMER! THAT DOG EATS RUBBER!

RUN!

DON'T STEP IN THOSE POTHOLES!

I'M MORE CONCERNED ABOUT MY REAR END!

AAHHHHHHH!

SQUISH!

OH, WINNIE THE POOH!

WHAT?

I JUST STEPPED IN A BOOMER PIE!

WAS IT . . . FRESH?

WOOF!

DIDN'T YOU HEAR THE SQUISH?

DIDN'T HEAR, BUT I SMELL IT.

WOOF! WOOF!

EEEUUUUW

WOOF!

1:17 p.m.
Scene 28/TAKE 1
Bernie's Car Wash, Corner of Watchung
and Bloomfield Avenues

"You stink, Isabella." Jeffrey winces as he bends closer to my sneaker. "You really do."

I turn and toe my right foot on the cement as Jeffrey works the hose. "Is the you-know-what coming off?"

"A little. It's not easy."

"I didn't ask if it was easy. I asked if it's coming off."

"Cranky. Cranky. Cranky. You try getting Boomer's gift to lawn fertilizer out of these crevices."

Jeffrey aims the nozzle closer to the bottom of my foot, and the spray suddenly shoots up.

"Hey! You're getting my pants wet!"

"Isabella, cleaning smushed dog poop off the bottom of a sneaker is not as simple as you seem to think."

"I know. Sorry. You're doing a good job . . . I just don't want to be drenched to my knees, that's all."

"There. Done." Jeffrey drops the hose, and we watch a light-brown puddle grow around my feet.

131

I carefully step aside and sniff. "Done? Really? I think I still smell bad. Can't you use a little soap or something?"

Jeffrey sighs.

"I'm only thinking of you. You have to smell me. Besides, we can't sneak into the academy with me wearing dog poop perfume. If Mr. Hansen, the custodian, is walking around the building, he'll track down that scent before you even slide my mag stripe. Two weeks ago, after four exterminators couldn't find where an awful odor was coming from, it was Mr. Hansen who located three dead squirrels in the fireplace on the third floor. He's got a nose like a bloodhound. Trust me."

"All right. I'll get soap. Jeesh."

Jeffrey walks over to the tunnel where cars take their showers and talks to the kid in the jumpsuit who's in charge of the final dry wipes. He comes back carrying a bottle filled with green liquid and a clean towel. I roll up my pants midway to my knees, then turn and toe my sneaker as Jeffrey squirts detergent on the sole.

"It's as clean as it's going to get unless you've got a toothbrush on you—and if you do, forget it. I'm not going there."

Jeffrey wipes his hands on the towel, and I sniff. "Better. Thanks. Okay, then. Let's get out of here!"

He grabs me by the back of Auntie Ella's sweater.

"Hold it, zebra girl. Not so fast."

"What's the matter? *You* didn't step in anything too, did you?"

"No. I didn't step in anything," Jeffrey says, rolling his eyes. "But I'm starving. I ran over to your aunts' house right in the middle of a ham and cheese sandwich. I'm hungry, Isabella. How about we stop at Holsten's? It's right up the block. I have to eat."

"*Now?*"

"Hey, don't go rolling your eyes at me, Isabella Antonelli. I just cleaned dog doo off your sneaker and I'm about to save your life. Are you really in a position to deny me food? Brainpower needs nourishment. Aunt Minnie didn't even offer me a cookie."

"All right, all right. We'll stop at Holsten's on our way up to Fortier. But no wasting time. We'll get take-out."

1:21 p.m.
Scene 29/TAKE 1
Holsten's Ice Cream Parlor

We push through the door at Holsten's and are greeted by the aroma of burgers sizzling on the griddle and the odd combination of chocolate sauce and french fries. Nicky

Lombardo's bushy eyebrows lift clear to his low hairline as he smiles broadly from behind the black-speckled Formica counter.

"Look who's here!" With his hand over his head, Nicky drops a scoop of chocolate ice cream into a waiting fluted sundae glass. "Isabella! The YouTube star!"

"Great idea you had coming here, Jeffrey," I say under my breath while forcing a smile and a wave to Nicky as the small room erupts in applause from the dozen or so people sitting at tables.

"What are you complaining about?" Jeffrey whispers as I feel eyes watching my every step. "Being famous only means we get quicker service."

"Counter stools or back booth, kids?" asks Nicky, squirting circles of whipped cream into the glass and tossing a red cherry on top.

"Booth," I answer, pointing straight ahead and walking to our usual spot at the back of the restaurant.

We each slide onto our own side of the red leather banquette and inch close to the wall, trying to ignore the stares, while two people in booth five hold up their phones and take my picture.

"Menus or the usual, kids?" asks Marie, as I see lights still flashing from the corner of my eye.

"Pork roll with cheese for me, today. On a kaiser. No

seeds, please," says Jeffrey as Marie scribbles the order on her pad. "Can you add a pickle, too?"

"Naturally, sweetie. What about you, Isabella? How about a side of your favorite rings?"

"Sounds good," says Jeffrey, answering for me.

I roll my eyes at Jeffrey. "Marie? Can you please ask Nicky to make everything to go? We're in kind of a hurry."

"You got it, tootsie."

Marie slides the yellow pencil behind her ear and it disappears into a Brillo pad of gray hair. She stuffs the notebook into her white apron pocket and winks. "I'll put this on your tab."

I lean across the table and whisper to Jeffrey. "So? Do you think my idea will work?"

Jeffrey sighs. "Look, Isabella, all I'm promising is to hack into the site. After I get the phone number of that 'devoted' fan, it's still up to you to do a convincing imitation of Aunt KiKi and get the webmaster—whoever he or she is—to add the information."

I nervously play with the saltshaker. "You'll make sure Oakleigh sees it, right? You have to make her believe what is fake is true and what is true is fake."

"Relax. Didn't I say I would?"

"I knew I could count on my best friend."

He smiles. "I thought maybe you'd traded me in."

"Jeffrey, you know you're my best friend. You're just not my *girl* best friend. Having girl best friends is different, that's all."

"I get it," he says, checking his phone for any new messages. "Just make sure you make a full confession after the election. After all the work you said they've done on your campaign, they deserve the truth."

Three Weeks Ago
Oakleigh's House
Campaign Strategy Sleepover

"These posters are fabulous, if I do say so myself," Emory said, sitting cross-legged on her bedroom carpet, colored markers scattered around her. She held up the large cardboard rectangle, nodded, and smiled. "VOTE FOR ISA-BELLA: *Elle est authentique!*"

"Positively brilliant, Em!" said Anisha, jumping off the bed and reaching down for one of the dozens of others piled on the floor, then holding it up arms length in front of her. "I like this one too—ISABELLA FOR REAL. That should knot Jenna's shorts."

"I'll say," Emory agreed with a laugh.

"And don't worry about your speech, Isabella," Oakleigh said, giving a puff to each lens of her glasses, then wiping both with the bottom of her sweatshirt. "I'll work on it with you. Remember, we need to focus on not only the slogan, but your campaign promise too."

Emory stood up and cleared her throat.

"FORTIER ALL THE WAY! HONESTY. FRATERNITY. AND NEW GYM UNIFORMS!"

"Leave it to you, Isabella, to get down to the most common denominator," said Oakleigh. "New uniforms is an issue that cuts across every grade level!"

"That change in attire is something we painfully need and is woefully overdue," said Anisha. "Girls at Fortier have been wearing those dreadfully awful gray bloomers since the academy was founded in 1912. Isabella, your idea of neon biker shorts was simply aces. How ever did that inspiration of spandex float into your head?"

"Uhhhhh . . . who knows?" I said with a shrug. "It just sort of . . . came to me out of the blue, I guess."

"Blue! *That's* the color I need to use here," Emory said, grabbing a marker and getting back to work on the last poster.

Anisha sat down on the floor next to me and put her arm around my shoulders. "Isabella, do you think perhaps your mum might have her designers in Milan create a whole new look for us with our regular uniforms as well?"

"Mmmmm . . . *maybe*."

"How great would that be?" said Oakleigh. "I'm sort of tired of those neckties."

"Ditto on weary. You know something, ladies? I'm feeling famished," Anisha said, rubbing her stomach. "What say we raid your kitchen, Em, and find something to munch?"

"Food? I'm in," said Emory, capping the marker and tossing it aside. "Follow me, girls," she said, heading out the door.

The three of us followed her down the curved stairwell into the huge kitchen, where we all ran to the refrigerator and huddled around the open door.

"We have tons of yogurt, and here's half a melon."

"I'm afraid that looks to be a tad moldy," said Anisha.

"I agree," said Oakleigh, who was the scientist in the group. (I lucked out when she chose me for her lab partner, because I don't think I could have dissected that frog without her. At least not without barfing up my breakfast.)

"Wait a minute—I think we have frozen pizza somewhere," Emory said, pulling out the bottom freezer drawer.

"Why eat frozen pizza when we've got Isabella!" said Oakleigh.

"That's right," agreed Anisha. "Isabella, give us a preview of the eggplant parm you're going to make for the rally next week."

"You mean, make it . . . *now?*"

(I was still working on how I was going to convince Nonni to make two trays of eggplant parmigiana, and then bring them to school without her—or Aunt Rosalie—noticing.

"How lucky is this?" Emory said, rifling through the vegetable drawer. "My mom bought an eggplant! Isabella, you can teach *us* the recipe!"

"Uh . . ." I looked up at the clock. "Gosh, it's so *late*."

"It's ten o'clock! It's not even a midnight snack. Besides, this is a sleepover. We can stay up all night. Come on, make us your specialty," Emory urged.

"How do you start?" Oakleigh asked as she leaned against the big center island, her elbows resting on the granite.

"Start?" I said, staring at the big purple thing now in my hands. "Um. Well, with *this*, of course."

"Here's a knife," said Emory, pulling one from a block of wood on the counter. "Will this work for you?"

"Oh. Wait," I said. "What about the tomatoes? Do you have San Marzano tomatoes?"

"San who?" Emory said over her shoulder as she opened the double pantry door. "I'm not sure if we have a can of tomatoes with that name."

"Well, the sauce *really* should be made with those. It won't be the same using something else. In fact, sorry to

140

say, but it's just not worth the effort without using the proper ingredients. The most important thing in any recipe is good ingredients, you know."

Emory moved several cans on the pantry shelves and then she groaned. "Darn. All we have is one small can of chopped tomatoes."

"Yeah. Darn," I said, doing my best pretend groan. "Not going to work."

"So now what?" asked Oakleigh.

"Isabella, why don't you check out what else is in the fridge and whip something up?" said Anisha.

I took my time strolling back to the refrigerator and tried to think of something that was easy enough for me to cook and that I had seen Nonni make a million times. I pulled open the door, staring at the mostly empty shelves, and then tugged open the vegetable bin, where I saw three long light green peppers. Cubenelles. I smiled and turned.

"How about pepper and egg sandwiches?"

"Sounds yummy!" said Anisha.

"Good for me," said Emory, pulling out a large frying pan from one of the cabinets as I reached into the refrigerator for the carton of eggs. "Are these hoagie rolls okay?" she asked, taking a bag from the bread drawer.

"Perfect!"

I quickly began chopping the peppers on the wooden cutting board and nodded toward the bottle of olive oil near the cooktop on the far side of the island. "Pour some in the pan will you, Oak?"

"How much?"

"Just to cover," I instructed. I cupped the cut peppers in my hand and tossed them into the pan, then turned the burner to a medium flame. "Let them get all soft and sweet, and then I'll scramble in some eggs."

"Mmmm," said Emory, taking a whiff as the peppers sizzled. "Smells good."

I smiled. "Yeah. You can't beat pepper and egg sandwiches . . . unless we toss in some potatoes, too!"

Jeffrey is still scrolling. I pull a napkin from the dispenser and watch him read as I nervously fold and unfold the paper rectangle, making bad origami. Suddenly, a clean, flat napkin slides onto the tabletop next to my awful-looking paper sailboat, followed by the sound of a high, shy voice.

"May I have your autograph, pleath?"

I turn my head and see a little girl, her chin barely clearing the edge of the table, her smile showing off big dimples and two missing front teeth.

"An autograph? From me? Really?"

Her blond curls bob with repeated nods. I look across the room and see her parents waving at me from three booths away.

"Uh, gosh. Sure. I'll be glad to give you an autograph," I say, thinking of Aunt KiKi. "The thing is . . ." I reach into both of my pockets but come up empty. I look down at her and frown. "Sorry, I don't have a pen . . ."

A black Sharpie flies over my shoulder from the booth behind us and drops on the table.

"Here."

I don't need to turn around to know who said that.

I recognize that voice.

Frankie Domenico.

1:30 p.m.
Scene 30/TAKE 2

I uncap the pen, scrawl "Isabella" across the napkin, then hand it to the little girl before the *a* begins bleeding into the *l*. She gives a polite thank-you and is heading back to her parents when Frankie climbs over the banquette. He slides his butt down against the back of the leather bench until he lands with a plop, sitting so close to me, our shoulders touch.

"What do you think you're doing?"

"Nothing much." He leans back and folds his arms in front of his chest. "Feeling hungry, I guess."

"Well, feel hungry somewhere else. Preferably out of state."

Frankie laughs. "Hostile environment on this end."

He slides off the seat and then crosses over to Jeffrey's side of the table. "Thing is, Isabella, I'm feeling hungry right here. Right now. In fact, feeling like a double burger

144

and an order of fries." He pats his stomach. "Chocolate shake, too."

He takes off his baseball hat and pulls it down over Jeffrey's forehead. Jeffrey takes off the hat and tosses it on the table in front of Frankie.

"Isabella and I are busy, Frankie, so . . ."

I put the cap on the marker and roll it across the table. "Take your pen and *go*."

Frankie rolls the Sharpie back to me. "But I'm *really* hungry, Isabella, know what I'm saying? And since I'm going to have to walk *all the way* back to your street to show that news lady with the blond hair this great picture I took of Jeffrey and *you* being chased by Boomer—"

"You took a photograph of us?" Jeffrey asks.

Frankie puts his hand in his pocket and pulls out his phone. "A pretty good one, too, if I say so myself—considering I'm what you call one of those amateurs. You want to take a look at yourself from *behind,* Isabella?"

"Not really," I say, picturing myself trying to climb over that fence.

Frankie grins. "Hey, how's that penthouse of yours, Isabella? And that castle you're always flying off to in your 'Mom's' private jet. Where is it again? Scotland? Ireland? I forget. I wonder if your new best friends can fill me in on that? . . . Whaddaya think?"

145

Jeffrey shakes his head. "Blackmailing for a burger is low, Domenico. Even for you."

Frankie laughs as he pockets his phone. He puts his hat on backwards and grins, looking at me from across the table.

(How anybody even *thinks* that human being is cute is a mystery to me. And his eyelashes are not that long. They aren't.)

Marie walks over to the booth, and places our take-out bag on the table. Frankie winks at me and gives his burger and shake order. As soon the pad is in her apron and Marie is heading for the grill, I stand and motion to Jeffrey.

"Let's get out of here. Take *him* with us."

"You're kidnapping me?" Frankie says as Jeffrey nudges him out of the booth.

"Are we, Isabella?" asks Jeffrey, wide-eyed.

I look at Jeffrey. "We can't leave him here. He knows too much." I take a step and go eye to eye with you-know-who. "And I can't trust *him* to keep quiet."

"Hey, what about my food?"

I turn toward the counter. "Excuse me, Marie. Put that last order on my tab and give it to your next customer."

"You got it, sweetie."

I nod to Jeffrey and point at the take-out bag on the

table, but Frankie grabs it before Jeffrey has a chance. He grins and stuffs it into the pocket of his hoodie.

"Where are we going?" he asks with a smirk.

"You'll find out," I mutter as Jeffrey hustles him past the row of leather booths and gives him a poke in the back as we all exit. "You got a problem with that, Domenico?"

He smiles at me, showing off that dumb-looking dimpled chin.

"Me? No problem at all, Antonelli. Where you lead, I follow."

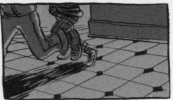

WHAT HAVE YOU GOT IN YOUR POCKETS?

TWO PAPER CLIPS AND A PIECE OF GUM.

NOTHING BUT MY ID. AND . . .

ALINT ELLA'S LIGHTER.

GIVE ME THE GUM.

PAPER CLIPS.

ISABELLA-- GIVE ME SOME LIGHT.

WHAT'S THE GUM FOR?

I ATE ONION RINGS, REMEMBER? DON'T WANT TO OFFEND.

CLICK!

IS THIS BREAKING AND ENTERING?

ONLY ENTERING.

2:10 p.m.

"Wow! Look at this place! It's Computerland!"

I glare at Frankie as the three of us walk into the room filled with rows of desks topped with computer monitors. I point my finger to his chest. "No talking. No touching. No nothing."

Jeffrey pulls out a chair and sits in front of one of the monitors in the back of the room. Frankie grins, then blows a bubble and swaggers to the other side of the room.

"Swipe your ID, Isabella," Jeffrey says. "Looks like the system here uses a wireless NIC card, so I just have to get the router to reboot. Once I figure out the administrator's code, we'll be in business. Don't worry. That's an easy hack."

I walk over to Jeffrey and reach into my pajama pants for the card. I swipe the mag stripe and his fingers fly on the keyboard.

"Open Run and enter cmd . . . net user/add, type a username, space . . . my favorite, easy-to-remember pass-

151

word—WozniakWonk—enter it into the prompt, and log off. Now I can log on to the Internet without anyone here at Fortier knowing, because I'm the administrator with full Internet-access privileges."

"Hey, Jeff? You talking English?"

I spin around to Frankie. "Shhhhhhhh!"

He cracks his gum. Grins.

We hear a *bing* and the monitor lights up.

"We're up!" says Jeffrey, leaning in to the computer screen. "Now, let's see . . . C-O-N-T-E-S-S . . . A. Here we go! Here it is. Top site. This has to be the one the girls were talking about."

I look over his shoulder and stare at the image on the screen. "Oh my gosh! There's the set from *Search for Truth, Lies and Love*! Wow. Look at Aunt KiKi," I say, pointing to the photo of her dressed in a pink gown, dripping in fake diamonds, with triple long black lashes stuck on her half-lowered eyelids.

"Start practicing your best imitation, Isabella. It won't take long for me to figure out the identity of your Contessa worshiper. Then you can make that call and we can get out of here before somebody catches us."

The screen fills with numbers, letters, and symbols running side to side. Vanna White wouldn't even know these combinations of consonants and vowels.

Jeffrey laughs to himself. "How short is this WPA password? Too easy! Lazy, lazy webmaster person."

"Hey, Isabella?" Frankie calls. "Come here. Got a question for you."

I squinty-stare like Aunt Minnie. "I thought I asked you not to talk."

He blows a pink bubble then raises his hand.

I sigh. *"What?"*

He sucks in the deflated bubble, snaps, and chews. Loudly. "Can you swipe this computer over here so I can play Zombie Balloon Heads?"

I double-squinty-stare.

"Monkey Quest? . . . Papa's Pancakeria?"

"Quiet! Jeffrey is concentrating. And get your feet off the furniture!" I say, hitting his sneakers.

Frankie leans back against the wall, balancing the chair on two legs. "I expected more *gratitude,* Isabella. After all, who was the one who saved your 'tortellini' and got you in here?"

I hate to admit it, but we couldn't have done it without him. "Okay. I'm"—I swallow and shiver as the word leaves my mouth—"grateful."

The chair clunks down on all fours, and Frankie smiles. "Nice."

"But keep quiet."

"Not nice."

"Getting close, Isabella!" Jeffrey calls from the other side of the room. "This was easier than I thought."

"Whoa. Whoa! Stop," I say, looking at you-know-who. "What do you think you are doing?" I step forward, hands on my hips. "What's in your hand? Do not tell me you are writing *my* name on *your* arm with that *black marker* . . . Are you? . . . Well?"

"You said don't tell."

"Push down those sleeves! You better hope that ink is washable."

Frankie laughs. "Or what?"

"Almost there!" cries Jeffrey from behind the monitor. "Just cracked his WPA keys!"

"No way is that English," Frankie says as I run up to Jeffrey.

I crouch next to Jeffrey's chair and stare at the screen. "We're lucky," he says. "The person we're looking for is somewhere in the Northeast."

"Really?" I say, wondering how he figured that out when the screen looks like a Scrabble game gone awry.

"Wait a minute—wait a minute—this person is right here in New Jersey . . . Whoa!"

"What, whoa? Whoa, what?" I say, watching Jeffrey type like a wild man.

"The location is coming up. I don't believe it . . . It says *Belleville.*"

"Belleville? As in Belleville, New Jersey? Our Belleville, New Jersey?"

"On our street!"

"Broadhead Place?"

"That's what this says: four thirty-five." Jeffrey turns away from the screen and looks at me. "Four thirty-five? Who lives at four thirty-five?"

I begin picturing every house on our block. "Mr. Colandra is across the street at four twenty-seven. The Fazekas are at four thirty-one . . . Four thirty-five is . . . *Mrs. Kostopoulos?*"

"No way!" says Jeffrey. "Can't be. Mrs. Kostopoulos is your Aunt KiKi's devoted fan?"

I feel a tap on my shoulder. I turn and Frankie grins.

"We are busy here! What do you want?"

"I want to help, that's what."

"You? Help?"

"I'm not kidding, Isabella. I have some pertinent four-one-one to relay to you."

I roll my eyes. "Uh-huh. And what sort of 'pertinent' information would that be?"

"That devoted fan is not Mrs. Kostopoulos . . . It's *Bobby.*"

We cut through the Murphys' yard on Molnar Avenue, which backs up to Broadhead Place. Frankie makes a detour down their kids' slide before the three of us squeeze between two garages and head out front to my street.

"Stop!" Jeffrey says, puffing, as the three of us run down the driveway to the sidewalk. "This is no good. We can't get to the house, Isabella. Look. The TV trucks are still on the street. Two of them are right in front of Mrs. Kostopoulos's house."

"But we have to get past them so we can talk to Bobby."

Frankie swings around the street pole. "If either of you two is interested, I might have an idea that could work."

I look over at Jeffrey, then back at Frankie. "And that would be exactly *what?*"

"We get you a disguise."

I sigh and look up at the graying sky. "A disguise?"

"That's what I said. Then you can walk right past those TV people and nobody will recognize you."

"Uh-huh. And just where would I get a *costume* right now?"

156

Frankie stops twirling around the pole and walks over, hands in pockets. "I'm not talking a *costume,* Isabella. I said disguise. And *that* you can get from me."

"You?"

"That's right, me. And Jeffrey. Between the two of us, I think we can change you into a guy."

I put my hands on my hips. "A boy? Excuse me, but nobody is going to believe I'm a boy."

"Wait a minute, Isabella," says Jeffrey. "I think Frankie's got something."

"Jeffrey Levandowski, are you saying I look like a boy too? Listen, just because I don't exactly have the same shape as Emory doesn't mean I can pass for a—"

"Take it easy. Nobody is saying you look like either of us, but I think Frankie is onto something."

"Oh really?"

"Look, you want to get to Mrs. Kostopoulos's house, don't you? Well, nobody is going to pay attention to three eleven-year-old boys when everyone is looking for a girl. So take off that zebra sweater and put on my shirt."

"This too." Frankie tosses me his hat. "Hide your hair under this."

I put on Jeffrey's checked shirt, then push my hair under the cap. Frankie bends down, picks up the striped sweater, and chucks it behind the bushes in front of the house on the corner.

"Hey! What are you doing? That's my aunt's favorite sweater!"

"Don't worry. It's safe," says Frankie. "Nobody is swiping a sweater that makes you look like a zebra. We'll get it later." He stands facing me. "So let's see what what we've got here. What do you think, Jeff?"

"Mmmmm. I don't know. She needs something else."

Frankie drapes his arm around Jeffrey's shoulder and nods. "Yeah. I think you're right."

Jeffrey places his wire-rims on the bridge of my nose and Frankie grins.

"Sweet."

"If it's okay with the Hardy Boys, can I go now?" I say, heading up the sidewalk.

Jeffrey grabs my arm and pulls down the bill of the cap. "Remember not to walk like a girl, Isabella."

"Yeah. Give it some swag. Cool-ability. Just follow my lead. Can you do that?"

I stare at Frankie over Jeffrey's glasses. "I think I can figure it out."

Frankie laughs. "Just asking."

I keep my head down as we walk past the hot dog truck and the aroma of those "all-the-ways."

I'm afraid Manny will recognize me, as he's been seeing my face along with Uncle Babe's almost every Tuesday since I was four (which is when Mom stopped being afraid I would choke on a hot dog).

Looks like Frankie was right. The disguise works. The three of us make our way through the crowd without anybody even turning their head. We get to the Kostopoulos house and Frankie leads the way down the driveway and then around to the back of the house.

"I'll do the talking," says Frankie, pushing up the sleeves on his hoodie as we all step up to the back door.

"*You* will be quiet," I say, giving him back his hat and then handing Jeffrey his glasses. I nudge Frankie aside and knock on the door.

"Isabella, Bobby and I are tight. He umps my ball games. He's a good guy. Let me talk to him."

I poke a finger in his chest. "No. And spit out that gum."

"It's still got flavor!"

"Spit."

159

Frankie rolls his eyes and reaches for the wrapper in his jeans back pocket. He takes the gum from his mouth, rolls it up in the paper, and stuffs it back in his pocket.

"She's tough. Very tough," he says, turning to Jeffrey. "Lucky for her, I like tough."

"Shush!" I say just as Mrs. Kostopoulos opens the door.

"Oh my goodness! Isabella, is that you?" She primps her cemented hair and unties the flowered apron from her waist. "Our neighborhood star! Goodness gracious!"

"Hi, Mrs. Kostopoulos. How are you today?"

"Wonderful. Wonderful!" She opens the door wider. She smiles and with both hands smooths wrinkles from her cotton housedress. "Come inside! Everybody. Jeffrey. Frankie. Sit. Let me get you kids a soda or somethin'."

Frankie pushes me aside. "Thanks, Mrs. K. I could go for a—"

I grab him by the bottom of his sweatshirt and pull him backwards. "Thank you, but we're fine, Mrs. Kosto-poulos. We don't need anything."

"How about a piece of candy? Look at all that I got here ready for the trick-or-treaters." She takes a basket from the kitchen table and Frankie grabs a Tootsie Pop. "Sure, have some candy while we visit."

"Actually, we're here to see Bobby," I say as Frankie unwraps the lollipop and sticks it in his mouth. "The three of us were wondering if we could talk to Bobby."

"Robert? Oh, dear." Mrs. Kostopoulos says chewing on her long, red-polished thumbnail. "You want to talk to my Robert?"

I nod. "Can we? Could we?"

"I don't know," she says, chewing and thinking. "He never sees anyone while he's working."

"We *really* need to talk to him, Mrs. Kostopoulos. It's very important."

"Life and death!" says Frankie, the round pop bulging from one of his cheeks.

Jeffrey and I turn and do a double squinty stare.

Frankie takes the pop out of his mouth and gives it a lick. "Make that . . . just life."

"Well," Mrs. Kostopoulos says with a heavy sigh, "he's very busy. He's in his office right now."

"His office?" I say, craning my neck for a peek into the living room.

"No, no. He doesn't work in there, sweetie. Robert's office is in the garage out back." She grabs a sweater from a hook on the wall. "I can't promise he will see you, since you don't have no appointment or nothin', but come. Follow."

Mrs. Kostopoulos throws the bulky woolen gray sweater over her shoulders, her slippers flapping and snapping as she leads us across the weedy backyard. We reach the side of the stucco garage and Mrs. Kostopoulos knocks on the small window covered on the other side by a pulled-down shade.

"Robert, dear?" she says, mouth against the glass. "Some people want to see you."

"I don't know any people I want to see, Ma," comes a deep voice from inside the garage. "I'm busy. Go away."

Mrs. Kostopoulos puts up one finger, telling us to be patient. "He's the sensitive, creative type," she whispers.

"But, Robert, dear, it's Isabella."

"Don't know any Isabella. Don't want to know any Isabella. Not interested, Ma."

"Isabella from across the street."

"Bye, Ma."

Mrs. Kostopoulos shrugs. "See? What did I say. He cannot be disturbed."

Frankie pokes me in the back and I turn around to see him with his arms folded and the lollipop sticking straight up from the side of his mouth like a five-inch toothpick.

"What now?" I whisper.

162

Frankie takes the pop from his mouth. "Let me handle Bobby. Like I said before. I got hidden talents."

2:50 p.m.
Scene 34/TAKE 1
Bobby's Office
(AKA: The Kostopoulos Garage)

Frankie holds the lollipop with one hand, knocks with the other. "Hey, Bob! Open up. It's me, Domenico!"

"*What?* Are you kidding?" The door swings open. "Hey! My boy, Frankie!"

All six feet three inches, three hundred pounds of Big Bobby Kostopoulos swallows Frankie in a bear hug.

"Domenico!" He takes off Frankie's cap and ruffles his dark, wavy hair. "Come on in!"

Frankie motions for Jeffrey and me to follow, and the three of us step inside.

"It's okay, Ma. I love this guy!" He gives Frankie another bear hug and turns to me with a wide, gap-toothed smile. "What a shortstop! Some glove on this kid. He can hit 'em, too. Hall of Fame. Hall of Fame. Domenico is great. I told his dad, this kid is totally underrated."

Frankie looks at me and grins. I'm ignoring the dopey dimple in his chin because I can't take my eyes off Bobby's "office." How he got all the stuff, I don't want to ask, but except for the faint aroma of Pennzoil, everything is an exact replica of the Contessa's living room from *Search for Truth, Lies and Love*. From the lavender carpet and curved pink silk couch to the colored pillows, and each and every accessory including the pretend family photographs that sit on round end tables, it's all here in Bobby's garage.

Even the entire cinderblock back wall is unrecognizable, covered from side to side, top to bottom with a mural-size photograph of Central Park. (Looks like Bobby painted fake windowpanes. Didn't do a bad job, either. Aunt Minnie would be impressed.)

Leaning against the middle of the double garage door is a fake fireplace with a portrait of the Contessa above the mantel. Aunt KiKi never looked better. To one side is a large desk with a big computer monitor. I'm guessing that's where Bobby does his webmastering.

"Sit down. Relax," Bobby says, the pink cushion buckling into a *V* as he plops down on one end of the curved sofa. He pulls up the baggy knees of his sweatpants, then places his hands in back of his head of buzzed hair.

Jeffrey and I follow Bobby's lead and take a seat on the couch.

Frankie wiggles in between us, still sucking on his lollipop. He settles back and turns to me with a wide grin. I roll my eyes and ignore him by looking around the garage.

"I like your . . . office, Mr. Kostopoulos."

"Bobby. Call me Bobby," he says with nod. "Glad you like the place. Some people might think it's a little on the feminine side for a guy like me, but I was one of *Search*'s biggest fans. When the soap was canceled, it almost killed me. I was so depressed I couldn't get out of bed for a week. No kidding. But my mood brightened when I got lucky with some of my contacts in the city. I was able to pick up a lot of props from the original set for a song."

Bobby looks around the room and smiles. "I like the environment. Gives me inspiration."

Jeffrey nods. "Impressive. Especially your technical equipment," he says, gesturing toward the computer.

"Eh. That's only for the job where I make the big bucks. I consult for a few of the top Fortune Five Hundred on the Big Board, but the Contessa's website is what you might call . . . my passion." He sighs. "A lot of fans, including me, miss *our* story. Wasn't right that show ended before its time." He swallows hard and wipes away a tear.

Jeffrey arches an eyebrow as Bobby takes a handkerchief from his sweatpants pocket and blows his nose.

"So, kid," he says with a sniffle as he stuffs the handkerchief back into his pocket. "To what do I owe the honor of this visit?"

Frankie places his arm across the back cushion and I feel his hand slowly creep down to my shoulder. "Well, see, my friend Isabella here needs your help, Bob. Isabella is in a bit of what you might call . . . a jam."

Bobby leans his big frame against the back silk cushion and rubs the stubble on his chin. "A jam, huh?" he says as I brush Frankie's fingers off my arm.

Jeffrey slips his wire-rims into his checked shirt pocket and clears his throat. "You see, somehow, which we don't have time to fully explain and is way too complicated anyway, your website—which we think is a very well executed tribute site, by the way—is sort of responsible for causing a seriously messed-up situation. The site you created is so incredibly credible, Isabella's friends believe the Contessa is a real person, and that person is her mother."

"And because my cousin Vincent's videos went viral and I'm in them being me—as in 'for real'—my life as I know it is in the sewer . . . Get what I'm saying?"

Bobby stares.

"At my new school."

Bobby is still staring.

"With my new best friends."

"Who she lied to," says Frankie.

"Fibbed. I fibbed."

Jeffrey pushes his glasses up his nose. "Bob, all we're asking is that you alter a bit of information, which would get Isabella off the hook—temporarily—for being a fibbing, faking phony."

"Only one teeny, tiny change," I plead, clasping my hands.

"And once we make sure Isabella's friends have read it, you can hit delete, because she never really wanted to live a double life—"

"True. I didn't."

"And she wants to tell the truth about who she is—and she is *going* to tell the truth about who she is—"

"I am! Right after the election for sixth grade class president, because Jenna Colson is my best friends' mortal enemy and they are counting on me to beat her—and I think I have a good chance, too, because everyone loved the eggplant."

"Eggplant?" Bobby says, looking more confused than Auntie Ella.

"The thing is," Jeffrey says, "Isabella needs a *little* more time—which is where you come in, because you're the only guy who can give it to her, Bob."

"I am, am I?"

"Once her friends see, with your help, of course, that Isabella is an actress making a film in New Jersey with her brother, you can take that information off the site. Just as if it was never there! No harm. No foul. What do you say, Bob? I mean, Mr. Kostopoulos? Sir. Will you help Isabella out here so her friends won't hate her?"

"And I won't end up swallowing Palmolive?"

"Will you?"

"Will you—can you—won't you? *Please?*"

Bobby smiles his wide, gap-toothed smile and chuckles. "Wow. That is some story."

"You're telling me," says Frankie.

"Then you'll help us?" asks Jeffrey.

Bobby looks at me and grins. "No."

2:59 p.m.
Scene 35/TAKE 1

"*No?*" Jeffrey says in a pitiful voice.

"But, Bobby, you have to! You're my only hope!"

Bobby heaves a long, heavy sigh. "Would love to help you. *But,* I have scruples. I'm a professional, after all. I can't destroy the sanctity of the site and damage my credibility. Not to mention the responsibility I have to the Contessa and all her devoted fans around the world. I cannot put out information that will float forever in cyberspace when I know in my heart those words are fraudulent and not real."

"But the whole thing isn't real!" I cry. "Everything on that site is made up!"

Bobby puts his hands on his more than ample hips. "Excuse me, little girl? What words have just emanated from your lips? Did I hear *not real? Made up?* Because if that's what I think I heard—"

"Whoa-whoa-whoa!" Frankie shoves the lollipop stick into his hoodie pocket. "Let's not get excited," he says, putting his hands up. "Everyone chill. Cool the jets." He pokes me with his elbow and whispers in my ear, "Let me talk to him."

Frankie stands up from the couch and moves around the room, his arms gesturing wide. "Bob, picture the Macy's Thanksgiving Day Parade . . ."

"*What?*" Jeffrey and I both say.

"The Macy's Thanksgiving Day Parade," he says again. "Are you picturing it, Bob? The bands with all those trombones? Clowns? Floats? Big balloons coming down Broadway . . . Superman. Good ol' Snoopy. The Pillsbury Doughboy."

Bobby smiles. "Love that Doughboy."

"Well, here's the thing, Bob. That balloon is ready to pop. The question is, do we want the Doughboy to burst and leave a mess of himself all over Thirty-Fourth Street, or deflate *gradually*? Drifting to the ground, letting out air little by little so nobody gets hurt. What do you think?"

Bobby rubs the stubble on his unshaved chin again, and as he thinks, deep lines appear on his broad forehead. "I see where you're going with this, kid."

Jeffrey and I look at each other. "He does?" We look at Bobby. "You do?"

Bobby crosses one leg over the other and pulls up his white sweat socks. "In other words, the Doughboy is a metaphor for the mess in which Isabella finds herself now engulfed. And I, *moi*, the webmaster of all that is the Contessa, control the amount of 'air' in which the truth is to be released. Am I correct in this assumption?"

Frankie claps his hands. "There you go!"

Jeffrey leans closer to me and whispers, "I'm impressed. I didn't think Frankie knew metaphors."

"I didn't think he knew the word *assumption*," I whisper back. (I don't think *I* know the word *assumption*.)

"So, Bob," continues Frankie, taking a seat next to him on the far side of the sofa. "Would you help Isabella keep her friends? I mean, what's more important than having friends?"

Bobby sighs. His head goes up and down. And up and down. Down and up.

"No."

"No?" I cry. "But you have to! You just have to!"

Frankie looks at me with eyes widening and twists his hand to his lips, as if he is silently turning a key. "Bob, I see you want to help. I see you are . . . *struggling. Conflicted.* You're a reasonable guy. How can we make this happen for the good of *all*? What can we do for you to help change your mind?"

Bobby smiles at me and grabs Frankie around the neck. "Underrated. Didn't I tell you? This kid here is underrated! Totally underrated."

I sigh. "So, uh, what do you want, Bob? An autographed photo of the Contessa? *Personally* addressed to you? How's that?"

Bobby frowns and shakes his head. "A photograph? That's it? I've got plenty of those right here!"

Frankie stares at me and narrows his eyes. "Isabella, let us not insult a supreme webmaster with small-time stuff. The man needs something *special.* Perhaps arrangements can be made for a phone call from the Contessa to one of her most devoted fans."

"*The* most devoted," Bobby says. "Go on, kid. I like what I'm hearing. Keep talking."

"Or, say, a personal one-on-one *meeting* with the Contessa."

Bobby grins. "Getting warmer."

"*Dinner?* Dinner with the Contessa?"

Bobby rubs his chin.

"How about it, Bob?" asks Frankie.

"Mmmmm. I don't know . . ."

"With the Contessa's favorite fig and pear tart for dessert!" I blurt out. "Homemade *crostata di fichi e pere*!"

Bobby claps his hands. "Deal!"

3:10 p.m.
Scene 36/TAKE 1

"Thank you so much, Bobby!" I say as he walks us to the door.

"Thank my boy Frankie here," he says, giving him another bear hug. "The kid is totally underrated."

Frankie looks at me. "Hear that, Isabella?"

So maybe his eyelashes *are* sort of long.

Just don't get me started about that dimple on his chin.

3:10:25 p.m.
Scene 37/TAKE 1
Home

The three of us take the long way around the block back to my house. Jeffrey and Frankie walk me around the sticky bushes and garage toward my back door.

"Now remember," says Jeffrey as we get to the back porch, "as soon as Bobby calls me and says the info is up and running, I'll text Oakleigh. When I hear from her, you'll hear from me. Everything is going to be fine."

I sigh. "Sounds good. You're the best, Jeffrey. Thanks for helping."

"Yeah, I think we did it."

Frankie grins. "We did, didn't we?"

Jeffrey puts his arm around Frankie. "Let's go, Domenico. See you later, Isabella," says Jeffrey as he turns.

"Yeah, see *you* later," says Frankie, smiling over his shoulder.

I roll my eyes and head for the back door.

3:12 p.m.
Scene 38/TAKE 1

I open the door and step inside the kitchen.

I tap the front burner of the Norge for good luck and smile as I head downstairs for something to drink. An orange Gatorade would hit the spot. All that negotiating with Bobby made me thirsty. Hungry, too. I skip down the steps thinking even one of Aunt Rosalie's bricks might not taste too bad right now. I reach the bottom and turn toward the furnace.

I never make it to the refrigerator. Or that Gatorade.

My family is lined up liked bowling pins over at Bloomfield Lanes, with Vincent the headpin.

"Mind telling us here where you've been?" he says, arms folded. "I hope you know you ruined the interview with Channel Four."

"*Dahling!* What were you thinking?" gasps Aunt KiKi as Grandma begins sniffling and reaches for a box of tissues.

Aunt Minnie shakes a finger. "Rosalie is the cook all of a sudden?"

Nonni's hands are on her hips. "I can't believe you stole my eggplant!"

"Forget the eggplant!" says Ella. "Look at her! She lost my sweater!"

From this point on it's a jumble of voices talking all at the same time: "you said," "she said," "I can't believe you did what you did!" It's pretty much one of those big you-know-whats that I had a feeling was coming. So many tongues are clicking that the sound rivals cicadas.

The number ten pin is my mom.

She's the one person not saying a word.

She doesn't even look angry . . . but her eyes are shiny.

She looks sad.

She looks worse than sad.

"*Isabella* . . ." she says, in a voice barely above a whisper. "*What* did you do? . . . And *why* did you do it?"

Scene 39/TAKE 1
Attic Bedroom

Glug. Glug. Glug.

My life is pretty much down the sewer, and way stinkier than any story Poppi Flavio's cousin ever told. I finally came clean to Mom, Grandma, Grandpop, Nonni, Vincent, Aunt KiKi, Uncle Babe, Aunt Rosalie, and . . . well, you get the picture.

At least I was spared the Palmolive treatment. (Luckily we are out of Palmolive, and Nonni doesn't think a cake of Ivory tastes bad enough.)

I have no idea what Emory, Oakleigh, and Anisha must be thinking right now—I'll find that out tomorrow. Bobby never got the chance to add anything to the website. I know that from the one call I was allowed to make to Jeffrey before heading to my room for solitary confinement. Don't know much else, because I've been banished here for the rest of my life.

Well, practically the rest of my life.

Until I get a reprieve, Mom is calling it "an ongoing open sentence." (I never thought she could be tougher than Judge Judy.)

I toss my pillow to the foot of my bed, give it a punch, and lie down facing the wall. I put my hands behind my head and stare at the painting of Great-Great-Grandpoppi's farm in Pienza . . . I bet that little farmhouse was a *villa* to him and Great-Great-Grandma Lucia.

Looks like a villa to me, too.

Better than any penthouse or castle Contessa Monchetti was supposed to have, that's for sure.

I sit up and swing my legs over the side of the bed. I don't bother sliding into my slippers. I walk to the door and turn the knob. I'm breaking the rule, but I leave the room and tiptoe downstairs to the first floor. The house is dark except for the light coming from the TV on the jalousie porch.

10:35 p.m.
Scene 40/TAKE 1
The Jalousie Porch

"Swee' Pea!" Uncle Babe waves me in from the doorway.

"Watching anything good?"

He smiles. "Only getting interference tonight."

I sit next to him on the old futon, and his arm slips around my waist as we stare at the snow on the old set. My head finds just the right place against my uncle's broad chest, between his shoulder and the pocket of his flannel robe. He smells of tangerines and a Hershey bar.

He kisses the top of my head. "Had one of those days, did you?"

"Everyone hates me, Uncle Babe."

"Naahhhhh. Everyone doesn't hate you." He pulls me closer. "It's just that nobody around here *likes* you too much right now. But trust me, they don't hate you."

"Are you sure? Nonni is so mad, she burned dinner worse than anything you ever barbecued."

Uncle Babe gives a halfway grin. "Everyone might not like you, but remember, they still love you."

"They do?"

He hugs me. "Of course! You are part of them, they are part of you. Never forget that."

"Do you mean I'm a storyteller like Nonni, and have Aunt KiKi's eyebrows and Grandpop's nose?"

He chuckles. "Something like that."

I look up. "You don't think I'm going to inherit Nonni's beehive, do you?"

Uncle Babe's eyes smile, and he pats down the knot

of hair in the back of my head. For a long while we don't talk. We just sit quietly on the couch.

"Uncle Babe?"

"Hmmm?"

"I think everyone is disappointed in me."

He sighs. "It happens. When family loves like this family loves, they want the best for you. And they want *you* to be the best. Isabella, you can never be the best—not even good—if you pretend to be somebody you're not."

"Is that what you call philosophy, Uncle Babe?"

He pats my arm. "Sort of."

"I only wanted those girls to like me."

"You don't think they can like you for being you? Maybe you can give them a chance."

I sigh. "I think it's too late for that. Who wants a friend who is a fibbing, faking phony? I never thought those fibs I told would turn everything into such a mess. I never meant to hurt anybody's feelings, Uncle Babe. Honest. Especially"—it's hard for me to swallow—"Mom's."

Uncle Babe rubs his thumb against my cheek. "What do I always tell you?"

"Tell me?"

"You know. What does Popeye say?"

I sniffle. "'I yam what I yam'?"

179

"And?"

"'That's all what I yam'?"

He kisses my hair. "*You* is pretty good. Remember that."

10:56 p.m.
Scene 41/TAKE 1
On the Stairs (Again)

I leave Uncle Babe watching the snow fall and walk across the living room to the stairs. Frankie (*yes*, the cat) is waiting for me on the first step. He meows. I pick him up, and he nuzzles me under my chin as I carry him up to the second floor.

When we get to the top of the stairs, I don't turn for the third floor. I take a deep breath and head down the hall . . . to Mom's room.

10:56:18 p.m.
Scene 42/TAKE 1
Mom's Bedroom

My knuckles lightly tap Mom's door.

She doesn't answer.

I turn the knob, open the door just enough to pass through, and tiptoe into the room, Frankie still in my arms.

From the streetlight coming through the side window, I see Mom in bed, her back to me, facing the wall.

I walk across the carpet to the double bed and place Frankie near her feet. He circles twice then sits, tucking his front paws underneath him. I lift the flowered quilt and white sheet, then slip under the covers next to my mother. I put my head on the pillow and feel Mom turn toward me. Beneath the covers, her arm comes around my waist. She pulls me close.

I whisper into the pillow. "I never wanted a mom who is a contessa. I'm not making that one up, either."

She kisses me behind my ear.

"I think your real eyelashes are longer than Aunt KiKi's, too. Just saying."

Can a person be asleep when her eyes stay open all night?

The sun inches across Mom's bedroom carpet. I roll over and see that Mom is gone. She's probably in the bathroom getting ready to leave for the hospital and an early shift. I think about telling her and Nonni I have a stomachache and can't go to school, but I know the odds of that old excuse working are not in my favor. They sort of got wise to that one back when I was in second grade.

Breakfast is putting up a fight as I try to get it down. The corn flakes are limp and soggy waiting around in the bowl of milk for me to eat them.

Nonni points to the glass on the table.

Somehow, I manage to drink every drop of orange juice, but it isn't easy. Especially with Nonni standing right behind me.

Aunt Rosalie walks into the kitchen and jangles the car keys. It's the "long linoleum mile" as I make my way out of the kitchen, up the stairs, through the back door, across the drive, and into the back seat of the LeSabre. We hit every red light from our house to school, but it feels way longer with Aunt Rosalie giving me the silent treatment.

But as quiet as it was at home and in the Buick, my reception at school is anything but.

8:25 a.m.
Scene 44/TAKE 1
Fortier Academy

From the moment Aunt Rosalie drops me off in front of school, it's obvious most every girl, no matter what grade, has watched the videos or seen my face on TV. Walking through the foyer, I'm greeted with smiles, pats on the shoulder, thumbs pointing up.

"Hey, Isabella!"

"Saw those videos!"

"Cool!"

"Isabella! Everyone in my family clicked Like on the videos with your family!"

"You've got my vote tomorrow!"

A cluster of third-graders follow me up the stairs waving scraps of lined notebook paper, wanting my autograph.

As I head for the sixth grade lockers, Jenna Colson stops me in the hall, holding a bunch of lollipops.

"Pretty good last-minute move, Antonelli, being on TV and all," she says with a sly smile. "But the election isn't today. We'll see who wins tomorrow."

I don't care about tomorrow.

I only care about the three girls standing by my locker.

8:26 a.m.
Scene 44/TAKE 2

There's a whole lot of me saying, *Turn around and head for anyplace else in the building.* And there are some good places to hide, too. But one very tiny part keeps pushing my legs to the end of the hall until I'm standing only an arm's length from Emory, Oakleigh, and Anisha.

I look into their faces. "Hi."

"Hi," they say back.

I take a deep breath. "Sooooooo . . . guess you know I'm not who you thought I was." I swallow. "Who I let you think I was."

Anisha leans against her locker and fingers the end of her braid. "Pretty much."

Oakleigh pushes her glasses up her nose. "Jeffrey

184

called yesterday afternoon and told me the whole story, and then I told Anisha and Emory."

Emory shifts her weight from one foot to the other, arms folded, waiting for me to say more.

"I'm glad he talked to you. I wanted him to talk to you. All along—since day one, I really did want you to know the truth about everything and who I really was . . . but, I guess you could say I got a little . . . sidetracked."

"*Sidetracked?*" says Emory.

"*Seriously*, Isabella?" says Anisha.

"Completely off the track is more like it," adds Oak-leigh.

I swallow hard. "Yeah, that excuse does sound pretty lame, doesn't it?" I put my shaking hands behind my back and clear my throat. "Since yesterday all I've been doing is thinking about how a person explains to her three new best friends why she is a fibber, faker, and big phony."

"And?" says Emory.

"I haven't come up with anything good yet—not that there is anything good to come up *with* . . . except . . . sorry. I'm sorry. I am. I'm really sorry for letting you think I was somebody I'm not. And that's the truth."

The four of us stand facing one another for what feels like forever, not saying anything.

"We've been thinking too," Emory says, staring at her shoes.

"Actually, it wasn't *all* your fault," says Anisha.

"Especially since we got that rumor way wrong in the first place," Oakleigh says.

I swallow hard. "Thanks, but I went along with it." I take a deep breath. "So now you know everything there is to know. I'm plain old Isabella Antonelli from Belleville, New Jersey. My mom is not a countess; we don't live in a fancy New York penthouse, or a villa in Italy, or fly around the world in a private jet. Hey, I don't even have a bicycle—and Jeffrey will back me up on that one." I take a another deep breath. "I'm just me."

"*Me* is good," Emory says.

"We like that me. I mean, you," says Oakleigh.

"You do?"

Anisha smiles. "Girl, don't you know? You had us at eggplant."

8:28 a.m.
Scene 44/TAKE 3

Group hugs are good.

Two Months Later, Friday, 7:35 p.m.
Scene 45/TAKE 1
Nonni's Basement Kitchen

As Grandpop likes to always say when he takes me to Yankee Stadium, the place is packed.

And all decorated, too.

Aunt Rosalie dragged out her Christmas decorations and strung white lights across the ceiling in the basement. Even the Volkswagen furnace is lit up. (It looks good when it twinkles.)

Uncle Babe, wearing his orange plaid sport coat, is making like *Dancing with the Stars* with Mrs. Kostopoulos. Vincent's parents, Aunt Lucy and Uncle Jimmy, are doing their own imitation too as Aunt Rosalie's playlist of Frankie Valli and the Four Seasons blares throughout the house. Even my grandparents are dancing. Arguing with every step, but dancing cheek to cheek.

Auntie Ella has sprinkled glitter on her spiked hair— "It's festive!"—and is leaving a sparkling trail of red and green everywhere she walks.

"Somebody needs to follow her with a broom!" says Aunt Minnie with a chuckle.

Ella shakes her head. "I say sweep tomorrow— sparkle tonight!"

Anisha holds up her phone to take a picture of Jeffrey, Oakleigh, and Emory and is photo-bombed by Frankie. (That would be the cat.)

My mom even looks glamorous. She's actually wearing pointy-toed high heels and a black minidress that I have never seen hanging in her closet. Who knew she had such good-looking legs under those baggy hospital scrubs? No alabaster doorknobs on her.

"Toast! Raise your glasses, my dahlings!" Aunt KiKi says as everyone gathers around the kitchen table and Grandpop drains a second bottle of Asti Spumante. "To my *amahzzing* filmmaker nephew, Vincent, and my equally *amahzzzzzzing* and *talented* niece, Isabella! Congratulations! Ratings on the first show are in! It's a hit! Bravo! Brava!"

"*Cin cin!*" everyone shouts, clinking a hodgepodge of glasses from Flintstones and Archie jelly jars to Aunt KiKi's pink crystal champagne flutes she brought from her apartment especially for the occasion.

"WAIT! STOP!" Aunt KiKi suddenly shouts. "Pop"—

she says, pointing to my grandfather before anyone takes a sip—"You *did* fill Isabella's and her friends' glasses with *juice, non hai fatto?*"

Grandpop holds up the empty bottles of white grape juice and Pellegrino. "You can take that one to the bank!"

"Eat! Eat, everybody!" Nonni shouts as she nudges Aunt Rosalie out of her way and puts a second platter of eggplant and antipasti on the table. She wipes her hands on her apron, then hurries to the stove, where she drops fistfuls of spaghetti into two pots of boiling salted water.

"Mangia!" Aunt Minnie orders everyone, holding a stack of plates as her cat-eye glasses fog up from the wafting steam from the cooking pasta.

"Mmmm, I love this," Emory says, taking another bite of pink meat, which is rolled up tighter than one of Uncle Jimmy's cigars. "What is this called again?"

I laugh. "Bologna with Q-Tips!"

"Mortadella," Aunt Minnie says, handing Emory a plate filled with rolled provolone, prosciutto, and capicola ham. "The comedian over there," she says, nodding at me. "Eat. Eat, skinny little girl!" she orders Emory. "You're a toothpick like Isabella."

Auntie Ella whispers in my ear, "Minnie's gravy is in the front pot, and *her* eggplant is in the green dish. The red one has Constanza's." She stands back and winks. "Just so you know."

"Hey!" shouts Bobby Kostopoulos, standing near the foot of the stairs. "Look who's finally here! Kid! You're late! Where you been?" he says as you-know-who comes strolling down the stairs into the basement. "Look at him, will ya? All spiffed up in that jacket and tie! Underrated, this boy!" Bobby grabs Frankie in a hug with his own bright pink sport-coated big bear of an arm. "Underrated."

Frankie looks at me from across the crowded room and grins that dumb dimpled-chin grin.

Emory whispers, "You've got to admit it, Isabella. He *is* cute."

I roll my eyes and bite into a piece of provolone.

"Too bad about that election," Jeffrey says, handing Oakleigh one of Aunt Minnie's chopped olive bruschetta.

She shrugs. "It's closer than we've ever come to beating Jenna before. Isabella only lost by seventeen votes."

Emory bites the top off a breadstick. "That last-minute campaign promise about no tests on Fridays is what did us in."

"That and that last batch of lollipops Jenna and her crew gave out on Election Day," adds Anisha.

I lift my Pebbles glass and take a sip of sparkling grape juice. "Next year," I say as the bubbles make me burp, "we'll really give her an Eggplant War. I've been thinking . . ."

"Uh-oh," says Jeffrey. "That's dangerous."

"No, no, listen," I say as they laugh. "Not only should we use Nonni's and Aunt Minnie's eggplant parmigiana recipes, but Anisha can make her grandmother's eggplant curry, and Oakleigh's mom can teach us how to make her famous eggplant Szechwan style."

"What about me?" Emory asks.

"You're the French expert. Ratatouille, of course!"

We clink glasses. "To future Eggplant Wars!"

"Attention, my dahlings! Attention!" Aunt KiKi taps a spoon on her pink glass. She flips one end of her long pink shawl over one shoulder. "Our star filmmaker is making a speech!"

Grandpop drags a chrome-legged kitchen chair from against the wall, and everyone applauds as Vincent, camera in hand, steps up on the red-cushioned seat.

"Thank you. Thank you, everybody! If it weren't for all of you, I wouldn't be here!" We all laugh when Nonni takes a bow. "I want to say thanks again to all of you for being . . . well, you! And I especially want to give a big thanks to my cousin Isabella—the best little sister I never had! Oh, and the next time I make you famous, I'll give you a heads-up!"

You-know-who gives out a big whoop somewhere over by the furnace, and I feel my face turning as red as Aunt Minnie's roasted peppers.

"And yes, watch out! I'm filming tonight," Vincent says, holding the camera above his head. "But I promise—the footage is only available for private family screenings!"

"Or not!" I call out, and everyone laughs again.

"Me first, my dahling," says KiKi, making one of her usual dramatic poses as Vincent gets off the chair. "Left profile! Left profile. It's my *better* side."

"Vincenzo! Get a shot of my legs!" calls out Auntie Ella as she hikes her skirt above her knees.

"MOVE! EVERYBODY AWAY FROM THE SINK!" Nonni shouts, potholder mitts grabbing both handles of the biggest pot we have in the house. "I'M DRAINING MACARONI!"

Boiling water swishes through Nonni's colander, and the room quickly steams up, as Frankie Valli sings, "You're just too good to be true . . . Can't take my eyes off of you . . ."

Suddenly everyone becomes quiet.

Uncle Babe slaps his forehead. "Well, blow me down!"

"*Madon!*" cries Aunt Minnie.

Aunt KiKi gasps. "*Amahzzing!*"

"Mother of Mercy! I'm making my shocked face!" cries Auntie Ella, her jaw dropping.

"What's going on?" Emory whispers as all eyes stare at the person who just came down the stairs. She pokes my ribs. "Isabella, who is *that?*"

The dark-haired, handsome man walks slowly toward my mother. He stops in front of her. They stare at each other, and then his arms slowly go around her waist, and he pulls her close. Whoa. Am I actually watching my mother get kissed? Double whoa. My mother is kissing back! It's like something from *Search for Truth, Lies and Love!*

Emory pokes me again. "Wow! Who is *he?*"

"I have no idea," I say, trying to catch my breath as Vincent focuses the camera in their direction and starts filming. "But I . . . I *think* . . . No. Can't be. Not possible. Is it? . . . Vincent?" I say, tugging his arm as he zooms in on the lip-lock. "Is that my . . . *father?* What's happening?"

"Season Two, kiddo . . . and we are rolling."

FADE OUT

CAST OF CHARACTERS

Vincent Palumbo
Eggplant Wars tops the ratings. HBO signs the series for eleven more episodes.

KiKi Caruso
The Contessa returns! New producer brings back *Search for Truth, Lies and Love* on the Internet.

Bobby Kostopoulos
Accepts new position as Aunt KiKi's public relations consultant.

Aunt Minnie & Auntie Ella
A Best-Looking Legs contest is scheduled for New Year's Eve in Atlantic City. (Judge to be determined.)

Nonni
Star of new online ten-minute videos *Nonni's Macaronis*.

Grandma & Grandpop
Still debating who put the spoon in the fork drawer. (Industry buzz about a series spinoff.)

Uncle Babe
Just inked deal for advice talk show on satellite radio titled *Popeye, Me, and You*.

Aunt Rosalie
Crocheting a computer cover for Jeffrey.

Jeffrey
Helping Oakleigh "break the code" in sixth grade math.

Anisha and Emory
Working on their own family eggplant recipes. (Cookbook deal being negotiated.)

Frankie (the cat)
Getting his own Barcalounger.

Frankie (not the cat)
Still underrated.

Mom and . . . Dad?
. . . For real?

Other Books You May Enjoy